"Where's Oliver?" Daniella cried.

Daniella took off running, Zara at her heels. They pounded up the stairs and down the end of the hall, almost colliding with Sam as he plunged out.

His face was stark, eyes glittering feverishly. She knew before he said a word.

"He's not here," Sam said, terror thickening his voice. "Oliver's gone..."

Rocky Mountain K-9 Unit

These police officers fight for justice with the help of their brave canine partners.

D0187563

Dana Mentink is a nationally bestselling author. She has been honored to win two Carol Awards, a HOLT Medallion and an RT Reviewers' Choice Best Book Award. She's authored more than thirty novels to date for Love Inspired Suspense and Harlequin Heartwarming. Dana loves feedback from her readers. Contact her at danamentink.com.

Visit the Author Profile page at LoveInspired.com for more titles.

UNDERCOVER ASSIGNMENT

DANA MENTINK

LOVE INSPIRED SUSPENSE
INSPIRATIONAL ROMANCE

Special thanks and acknowledgment are given to Dana Mentink
for her contribution to the Rocky Mountain K-9 Unit miniseries.

LOVE INSPIRED® SUSPENSE
INSPIRATIONAL ROMANCE

Recycling programs
for this product may
not exist in your area.

ISBN-13: 978-1-335-55509-0

Undercover Assignment

Love Inspired
22 Adelaide St. West, 41st Floor
Toronto, Ontario M5H 4E3, Canada
www.LoveInspired.com

Printed in U.S.A.

Behold, I will do a new thing; now it shall spring forth;
shall ye not know it? I will even make a way in the
wilderness, and rivers in the desert.
—*Isaiah* 43:19

To Zara,
a woman of strength and grace and a warrior at heart.

ONE

Sam Kavanaugh rarely took the time to hike the boundaries of his remote Cliffside Lodge in southwest New Mexico, but worry compelled him into the sizzling summer night. Climbing to a perch on a high pinnacle of rock, he could see only a fraction of the three million acres of national forest that sheltered the Gila River. Mesas, canyons, hoodoos, cliff dwellings, the wilderness had it all and he relished the wonders...usually.

Tonight the molten July air felt menacing, the screech of a vulture overhead grinding his nerves. There was nothing evil lurking in the desert night that might threaten Sam, his young son Oliver, or the five guests currently residing with them. Or was there? Unease nibbled at his nerves.

He hadn't imagined the jimmied kitchen window, though nothing had been taken. A random opportunist looking for quick money, he'd decided. But then there was the strange noise from outside that had awakened him in the wee hours and sent him scouring the property at three in the morning the night before. Again, he'd found nothing to worry about.

"So why are you hiking around again doing more

clandestine reconnaissance for no concrete reason at all?" he muttered to himself. Feeling foolish, he climbed carefully down from his rocky lookout and took the path around the side of the main house.

Moonlight played off the adobe walls of the two-story, Spanish Revival style inn. It was beautiful, unique, like his late wife Hannah whose dream it had been. And Oliver, their three-year-old son, was lying safe and sound in his bed inside with their housekeeper keeping watch, Sam reminded himself. All was well, no cause for alarm. He should go back to the lodge and try to get a few hours of shut-eye before his morning duties kicked off.

But he couldn't. If he'd learned anything from his time in the army as an explosives ordnance technician, it was to listen when his instincts were clamoring. Unless his instincts had become unreliable from too many long hours managing the inn or the worries of being a single parent.

Doggedly, he continued on, beaming his flashlight at the flagstone walkway leading up to the storage shed tucked behind a cluster of pines. A smudged footprint showed in the dust. From a man's shoe? A woman's? His heart kicked up a notch. The print had to be recent, since he meticulously swept every inch of stone each morning.

It might be nothing. Perhaps one of the newly arrived guests, disoriented, had left the print while trying to find their way to the main lodge. He reached out for the knob, expecting to find it locked as he'd left it.

Instead it turned under his fingertips.

He should have backed away, but that hard, stubborn part of him, the one that had gotten him through basic

training and army deployments, seized hold. If he'd forgotten to lock the door, he deserved to feel stupid. If
he hadn't…he intended to figure out who was messing
with his property and they were going to be brought to
task. This was not just a lodge, it was his home, a fortress for him and his son against the world. He prodded
the door open with the toe of his boot.

Hairs on the back of his neck stood on end as he felt
the rush of air behind him. There was only time for
him to fling up an arm before a sharp pain exploded
in his skull. His last thought was of Oliver as the darkness overtook him.

Officer Daniella Vargas was still simmering as she
drove her rental car from the airport through Silver City,
New Mexico, and pulled off before the steep slope up to
Cliffside Lodge. From the back seat her Malinois, Zara,
rolled her eyes in Daniella's direction with her black
muzzle resting on the few meagre strands of what had
been a basketball net.

"It can't hurt to try one more time," she said to the
dog as she dialed. "And by the way, you know you
can't take Nettie with you on duty." Nettie had to be the
strangest dog toy ever, but Daniella had not been able
to get Zara to attach to any normal stuffed squeaking
critter before she destroyed them.

Besides, Daniella figured Zara had earned Nettie.
Before she was fully trained, Zara had leaped up and
ripped the net right off the rim after Daniella's basketball game at the community center, just for the fun of
it. Zara was saddened to part with her hard-won prize
and Daniella had let her keep it. Daniella took plenty
of grief from the other K-9 handlers over Zara's weird

plaything, but they all admired the dog's incredible athleticism. She didn't perform such feets anymore, since she had the beginnings of arthritis affecting one of her back legs, but she was still plenty agile enough to do her job.

The phone rang a few times.

Daniella's commander, Tyson Wilkes, sounded weary when he answered, but she put that out of her mind. "Hi, Sarge."

"Made it to New Mexico?"

"Yes, sir. I'm on my way to the Cliffside Lodge now." She hesitated. "I was thinking that maybe I could get some security protocols in place to prevent any further break ins, and check security in the kid's room before I return to the unit," she said. "A couple of days tops."

He cleared his throat. "Daniella, we've been through this. You're there for however long it takes. You're the logical choice for this assignment."

To be a nanny? A highly trained officer with a brilliant protection dog? Her teeth clenched. Because she was a woman? She would be more offended if she didn't know Tyson to be a respectful boss and a good man. He'd already explained his logical reasons. "But…"

"We're stretched a little thin here." There was an edge to his voice.

True. The Rocky Mountain K-9 Unit was small to begin with, a Denver-based mobile response unit under the auspices of the FBI. The officers and their canines were dispatched around the Rocky Mountain region when needed.

The K-9 unit was busy as bees in the springtime, as her adopted uncle Cal would have said. She kept her tone light. "Harlow likes kids. She would be—"

"We need her dog available, in case."

The gravity of that statement tamped down her ire. Harlow Zane's beagle was a cadaver-sniffing dog. Daniella offered a silent prayer that Nell's nose would not be pressed into service in the search for the baby the team had been frantically trying to locate.

Last April in Colorado, a torched car was discovered on a dark road leading to Rocky Mountain National Park. An infant car seat and pink baby blanket were found near the car—as was an unconscious woman, Kate Montgomery, who'd been in a coma ever since. But there'd been no sign of the baby. It was two steps forward and three back, investigation wise.

A few miles from the charred car, another vehicle was found in a ravine with the body of Nikki Baker, wearing a blond wig. Hairs from the wig matched those on the blanket found at the burned car. They'd determined that that Nikki Baker was the missing baby's mother, but what was the connection between the women? Why had Nikki been disguised? Running? Was she another victim of an apparent serial killer who was targeting young women in the region? More questions than answers and the clock was ticking on finding Baby Chloe.

"Maybe…" she started.

He sighed. "Look, Daniella. I'm not going to force you to do this. Sam and I figured the best cover for you at the lodge was to pretend to be a prospective nanny. If you can get things under control quickly, you're free to leave." Tyson's obvious stress awakened her discomfort. She knew she could be abrasive, and he'd been supportive and a good mentor. The pressure on him was intense, worse, since a couple of incidents with the dogs had the FBI questioning his ability to lead.

Man up, Daniella. She inhaled, shoved her dark hair back from her shoulders and summoned her depleted supply of patience. "All right. I'll do what needs to be done."

"Thank you," Tyson said. "Sam's a good guy and he'll appreciate it. Besides, your uncle Cal is close, right? You can squeeze in a visit maybe."

"Sure. Thanks, Sarge. Talk to you soon."

She disconnected the call. Innkeeper Sam might be a good guy, but he obviously couldn't manage his personal business very well. What real threat could be brewing at a remote wilderness lodge in New Mexico? Not exactly a hotbed of intrigue. He was probably imagining something sinister in the shadows. He'd be better off equipping his son to face fears head-on. The little boy would feel safer if he knew he could protect himself.

It had worked for Daniella. She'd scraped and clawed to survive her childhood, but the struggle had forged her character.

Her deep well of tenacity had made her a good cop, and she would do her best for Tyson. If it meant reassuring a fretting single dad, she'd do it. After another steeply sloped mile, the Cliffside Lodge swam into view. Gorgeous, was her first reaction, the mellow gold of the structure glowing against a rugged backdrop of mountains. It was elegant and seemed to nestle into the landscape instead of competing with it. Not the rustic dive she'd been picturing. Surprise number one, she thought as she pulled into a tiny paved parking area.

"Leave it," she commanded as Zara snagged Nettie

when she opened the rear door. With a mournful look, the dog abandoned her toy in the car and leaped out, nose primed for new smells.

Clipping a lead to Zara's harness, Daniella walked toward a tall, muscular man with a closely trimmed coppery beard and mustache. He held a rake over his broad shoulder. He must be the groundskeeper or something. Fit, she thought. She kept her body as toned as she could, and she appreciated the effort it required.

She put Zara in a sit and greeted him.

"Sam Kavanaugh," he said, shaking her hand, his grip firm and confident. "You must be Daniella. Thank you for coming."

Surprise number two. Sam was not the geeky business owner she'd anticipated. This man looked every bit the sturdy outdoorsman. He wasn't even sweating in the late-afternoon heat. What's more, he had a nasty bruise discoloring his temple, which made it look like he'd been out grappling with bears or something.

"From the attack?" she said, pointing.

"Yes. Hit from behind and knocked forward into the doorjamb. So much for my catlike reflexes." He looked pained. "Listen, I wouldn't have called in a favor with Tyson, but I was low on options." He flushed. "There aren't many things I figure I can't take care of myself."

She shook her head. "Doesn't matter. I'm here. Tell me everything. I'm sure we can button this up quickly."

He took her to a patio area tucked in the shade of a couple of trees. It was still hot, but tolerable. A small boy sat at the table, eating a cookie. He had his father's broad cheekbones and caramel eyes, a glint of copper in his sandy hair.

"You were supposed to wait for the cookies, Oliver," Sam said.

Oliver offered a chocolate-smeared grin. Daniella hid her own. As a kid, she wouldn't have waited either.

"This is Ms. Vargas and her dog...er..."

"Zara," she offered. "You can call me Daniella."

Oliver looked at the large Belgian Malinois with her black muzzle and black-fringed ears. The little boy didn't seem at all frightened by her.

Sam waved Daniella into the chair. She declined the cookie. Charming as Sam and his kiddo appeared to be, she was in business mode. Anything to make this assignment move along faster.

Zara obediently settled at Daniella's feet, but she knew enough about her canine partner to understand the excited prick of the ears and the low lashing of the tail. Zara was hoping for one of the three things she adored the most; work, play or something to chew on.

Sam turned to his son. "Ms. Vargas—I mean Daniella, is here to help me take care of you for a little while, Ollie." The statement seemed to cause him discomfort judging from the tightening of his mouth. Like he'd said, he wasn't used to asking for help. Sam handed his son a paper napkin. "I need you to tell her what you told me."

Oliver was staring at the dog. "Cookie for him?" he suggested.

"No thanks, and the dog is a girl," Daniella said then realized her tone wasn't the warm-fuzzy type you were supposed to use around children. She tried again. "Chocolate will make her sick."

Oliver's eyes widened. "Oh." He shot a wide-eyed look at the cookie in his hand as if it were a time bomb.

Great. She'd already traumatized the kid. "Uh, just

because she's a dog. Chocolate cookies are fine for humans," she hurried to add.

In spite of her reassurance, he squinched his mouth and put the cookie down, picking up his plastic dinosaur.

"This morning, son," Sam prompted. "Tell Daniella what happened."

Oliver began to wrap his paper napkin around his dinosaur. "A bad man came into my room."

"Did you see their face?"

He shook his head.

Could have been a nightmare, Daniella thought, or his imagination. There was a reason youngsters made notoriously bad witnesses. "Was the person tall or short?"

"Tall."

Everybody probably seemed tall to a pint-sized boy. She looked at Sam. "Maybe it was your father come to check on you."

Oliver shook his head. "Nuh-uh."

With a friendly smile in place, she asked him gently. "How can you be sure, Oliver?"

Oliver continued to twist the napkin around his toy without answering.

After a few silent moments, Daniella looked to Sam. "I'm going to let Zara sniff around, okay?"

He nodded.

Zara leaped to her feet, ears and eyes swiveling to take in the surroundings. Sam followed her and Zara into the tiled courtyard, meticulously landscaped with pots of native plants. She eyed her excited Malinois. She'd have to make sure Zara knew she would not be allowed to excavate a nice hole for her ball during playtime. As a pup, digging had been one of the dog's many talents, but every so often her youthful tendencies would still peep out.

"You see why I'm worried?" Sam said as Zara checked out the space. "Someone was in his room?"

She framed her response carefully. "I can understand a certain level of concern. But the attack at the shed could have been a crime of opportunity, someone trying to break in and steal things. Or Oliver may have been imagining it or making something up." She'd said it wrong, she realized immediately.

Sam straightened to his full height, a solid five inches taller than she was. "My son isn't a liar."

Making lots of friends today, aren't you, Daniella? "I wasn't saying that. Little kids say stuff, right? Use their imaginations and weave it together with things they've seen on TV. Happens all the time."

His mouth was still a hard line. "Know a lot about kids?"

The remark stung more than it should have. Now it was her turn to bridle as she stared back at him. "No, but I've done my share of interviewing them."

"Oliver doesn't lie," Sam repeated. "And he doesn't watch TV. My late wife and I agreed on no screen time until he was older."

The whole conversation was shifting into troubled waters. *Regroup, Daniella. Get it back on track.* "I meant no offense, Mr. Kavanaugh. I'm a cop and I'm telling you the facts. Kids aren't reliable." When he started to reply, she held up a palm. "But I will do as thorough an investigation as I can, and if there's an identifiable threat, I'll stay here and deal with it. Fair enough?"

The caramel of his eyes darkened to mocha. "Thank you," he said stiffly. He looked like he was about to add on to his clipped remark when Oliver got up from the table and joined them, his wary gaze on Zara, who wagged her tail.

He held up his dinosaur. "Like this."

The dinosaur's face was covered by the napkin, two poked holes for the eyes to look through.

Sam took the proffered toy. "What's this, son?"

"The bad man had one," the boy said.

Sam stared at the toy, uncomprehending.

"A mask," Oliver said. "He wore a mask."

TWO

"Lunch will be in a half hour. Dinner is at six," Sam told her later. "After sunset, the guests are invited to a dessert bar outside to star-watch. Let me know if you require anything."

Require... She could tell he was still snippy with her. Why it bothered her, she couldn't say. She was there as a cop, not to be the innkeeper's buddy. Then again, they'd both become edgy since Oliver's revelation that his visitor had been masked. It was possible the child had made it up or imagined it, but some deep-down instinct told her it was true.

Sam stood in the doorway of the cozy room he'd led her to, all painted in neutrals complemented by the colorful southwestern-patterned bedding.

"This one's vacant. Feel free to use it as you'd like," Sam said.

An empty room couldn't be good at this time of year. "I'll need info on your guests and any employees."

"Sure. I'll share whatever I have, which isn't much on the guests. The only paid staff is me and the housekeeper Mae, and a few temps who help with the grounds sometimes. John Payat is a handyman for me when the task exceeds my skillset and I pay him to take guests on tours and handle the shuttling when I can't. He's a local. Surly, but I've never had any trouble with him. As far as guests go, five checked in last week, but not at the same time."

So they'd all been on the premises at one time or another and could have participated in the attack at the shed. She clicked open a tab in her phone to make notes. "Have you picked up any information from the guest chatter?"

Sam frowned in thought. "Paul Zariya is in one room. He's a businessman from Santa Fe, I think. His sister, Ingrid Zariya, is next door. Ingrid was my late wife Hannah's dorm mate when they were in college in Germany. She said she'd always wanted to see the lodge Hannah talked about, so she and her brother made it a stop on their itinerary." His eyes went soft and sad. "Paul told me he's squeezing in some recreation around business he has to tend to in Santa Fe. He said he's never traveled with his sister before, but Ingrid convinced him he should join her since he was nearby. Whitney and Matt Poleman are a honeymooning couple at the end of the hall. They were married last week in Silver Springs and they're traveling to Europe soon, but they wanted a quick trip to celebrate. They're next door to Edward Reese. He's on a cross-country trip of some sort, though I haven't gotten the particulars."

"That's it? Only four rooms booked?"

"Unfortunately." Sam huffed out a breath. "Things have been slow. Four guest bedrooms occupied, plus Oliver's, which adjoins mine, and one empty." He surprised her with a smile. "Suitable accommodations for a prospective nanny and her dog, right?" He quirked a brow and looked over Daniella's shoulder. "Your partner seems to like the digs."

Daniella turned to see Zara looked excitedly around the room. "She's an eager beaver...for a dog, but she knows who the boss is in our partnership, otherwise we'd be battling all the time."

He laughed; a pleasing baritone chuckle. "Kids are like that, too, from my limited experience. If you don't let them know who is the decision maker, they will assume they are. Before you know what hit you, it's cookies for breakfast and preschool all-nighters. Chaos all around." He raised a brow. "Is, uh, it is safe to have Zara around Oliver and the guests?"

Daniella nodded her head at the sleek canine. "Completely. She has a strong will, but she would never use aggression on anyone unless I gave her the order." She paused. "Or if someone was attacking me. My uncle tried to give me a bear hug a short while after I got Zara. She wasn't fully trained yet and she thought he was hurting me. She didn't bite, but she raised such a ruckus my uncle was afraid to hug or come near me for months. He still gives Zara that questioning look."

"Good to know. No hugs without permission." Sam ducked his head as if embarrassed by his remark. "I've gotta get going on meal prep."

"You're the cook, too?"

"And chief bottle washer, as Hannah would have said."

Another awkward silence. "I'm sorry for your loss, Mr. Kavanaugh."

He shook his head. "The name's Sam. I've learned to live with a missing piece. The trouble is I don't know how to keep her alive for Oliver. I'm afraid he won't

know his own mother." He rubbed a hand over his beard
and diverted his gaze.

Tragic that a cherished child would not know the
mother who'd wanted to love him. Daniella's own
mother did not have much desire to know her child,
gripped as she was by addiction. She imagined Hannah
was the exact opposite. The kind of mom who would
have sung to her son, cut his sandwiches into dinosaur
shapes and taught him to write his name. She shifted,
unsure what to say. Protection was her strength, not
nurturing, and definitely not parenting. No, certainly
not that. Her fingers went to the slender chain around
her neck as she tried to figure out how to reply.

He saved her by giving her a nod, turning before he
shut the door. "Please do whatever you need to. Look
anywhere you want. We have no secrets here."

But if someone was prowling the property and his
attack wasn't random, there were secrets Sam obviously
knew nothing about.

"And please do call me Sam," he added. "Everyone does. I should also tell you there's a cat lurking
around somewhere. His name is Midnight, but he never
comes when called. Figured you and Zara might need
to know that."

When he left, she looked hard at Zara. "Did you hear
that? A cat, and I'm sure it does *not* want to be your
friend no matter how hard you try, got it?"

Zara simply wagged her tail.

Daniella decided it would be best to start in Oliver's
room. The boy wasn't there, having followed his dad
downstairs to help in the kitchen. His bed, inexpertly
made, was obviously the work of a three-year-old. Daniella figured she would probably never be in a position

to raise children, but if her brother ever did, she hoped
he would assign chores to her niece or nephew like
Sam did. She should spend more time with those two
kiddos, though her dealings with her brother felt awkward. He was married, a good father with a supportive spouse; glaring examples of how well he'd fared in
his foster situation and what a mess hers had been in
contrast. It wasn't jealousy she felt when she compared
their lives. She was making her own way, and she was
proud of herself. Perhaps it was more of a quiet grief at
what could have been.

Casting aside the thoughts, she explored the small
space, a twin bed covered by a wrinkly dinosaur com-
forter, a dresser sporting a series of dinosaur figures,
a pad of paper on a turtle-shaped table and a colorful,
shaggy rug. Zara set about sniffing every square inch
of the room while Daniella went to the window. They
were on the second story, looking down into the landscaped courtyard she'd been in earlier. She tested the
window. There was a safety lock that would be easily
unlatched from the inside by an adult.

She was turning around when a stocky man with
thinning hair poked his head in.

Zara riveted her gaze on him immediately, still and
waiting.

"Oh, uh, hi," he said, glancing at the dog. "I got the
wrong room again." He cocked his head. "Isn't this the
boy's room? Oliver?"

"Yes. I'm interviewing for a nanny position." Daniella hoped her smile was suitably sweet. "I'm Daniella.
You're a guest?"

"Yep, sure am. On a cross-country trip from here
to the Carolinas."

"Super. What have you seen so far?"

He laughed. "Started in Santa Fe, so not much." He inhaled. "I'm gonna go snap a few photos of the garden for as long as I can stand the heat. Catch you later."

She noticed he had not given his name. Must be Edward Reese, she thought, recalling what Sam had told her about the guests. Had he accidently entered the wrong room?

She didn't think so for a minute.

Edward had intended to sneak into Oliver's room.

The question was why.

Sam fumbled to find the right key to lock the door of the old lodge and tried to keep his impatience in check. It was turning into a royal pain to be sure the shed and all the outbuildings were kept locked at all times. Retrieving the table linens from the old inn across the property, which they now used as storage and office space, had taken longer while he'd fussed with the locks. A time-waster, but the trouble would be worth it now that he'd fetched the crisp southwestern print napkins that would accompany the breakfast in the morning.

As he strolled from the tiny, antiquated old building to the new, he noticed Daniella and Zara peering down from the second-story window. He wished he hadn't gotten off on the wrong foot with her when she'd been merely doing her job. She thought he was overprotective, no doubt, defending his son when she'd suggested he'd been making things up. Even she'd seemed convinced when Oliver had told them the intruder was wearing a mask. Ever since that revelation, his stomach muscles had been bunched tight.

Waving a hand, she raised one in return. He hurried

to enter the building and escape her observant gaze. Hanging the keys on the peg, he deposited the linens and finished the last of the lunch preparations. Oliver colored with chunky crayons at the butcher-block counter under Mae's watchful eye. Mae, Sam's housekeeper and all-around helper, had arrived late as usual, pink-cheeked, white hair flying. Sam could never be mad at the woman whose perpetual optimism and work ethic made up for her tardiness. He'd traveled some very difficult miles since Hannah's cancer was diagnosed, and Mae had been there through all of it.

"Sorry I was late," she sang out. "I was watching my taped soap operas and I got sucked in." She grinned at Oliver. "Guess what, dinosaur boy?"

Oliver offered a cheerful dinosaur roar.

"Very scary. I found a new triceratops at the dollar store yesterday, and I'll get it out of my car as soon as the meal is done."

"Yea," Oliver shouted, abandoning his dinosaur speak.

"Ready to help?" Sam said.

"Yes, sir." Oliver carried a bowl of butter pats to the dining table. The room had been recently painted, the buff walls contrasting with the dark-timbered ceiling. He followed Oliver, nudging the switch with his elbow to activate the wrought-iron chandelier, adding a platter of cold meats and cheeses to the marble-topped buffet. Fragrant golden rolls sat next to a crock of fresh-made butter. An orzo and tomato salad with feta completed the service for Ingrid, since she was a vegetarian.

Sunlight poured between the trees, spilling through the floor-to-ceiling windows, sparkling off the china and silver, the sweating pitchers of iced tea and lemonade. He felt a swell of pride as the guests began to congregate, commenting on the décor and food.

Daniella stood a bit apart, statuesque, her dark eyes taking in every detail of the room. She looked neither critical nor admiring. They had gotten off to a rocky start, but he was grateful that at least there was someone objective taking a look at the situation. Was it a situation? Or merely a crime of opportunity followed by a child's imagination running wild? *The mask was real*, he told himself again.

Matt and Whitney entered and sat immediately. Whitney braided her long blond hair with her fingers, while Matt folded his arms across his chest and stared at a spot on the placemat. No cheerful banter between those two. Trouble for the newlyweds?

Don't waste time over petty stuff, he wanted to tell them. It can all be over far too soon. The familiar ache came and went, leaving a wash of fatigue in its wake. Why had he blabbed his deepest concern to the no-nonsense cop anyway? The fear that Oliver would grow up without even the slightest connection to the mother who'd died when he was eight months old. It was none of Daniella's business, nor did she pretend to care.

It was his problem, one he hadn't been able to solve. Showing Oliver pictures of Hannah, video clips, admiring the blanket she'd quilted for her son, were not enough to stitch a missing mother into the fabric of Oliver's life. But the Cliffside Lodge would stand as a memory, wouldn't it? The place they'd sacrificed and toiled over? It would be Oliver's legacy from Hannah. With anxious eyes, he swept the room again, finding it perfect from the bright-colored flower arrangement to Hannah's simple wooden crucifix hanging over the fireplace. The lodge was everything, and it had to be made safe for his son.

Edward came in, forehead glistening with sweat, glancing at Daniella. Sam realized he was forgetting his host duties. "Everyone, this is Daniella Vargas," he said. "We're conducting a working interview, sort of, for the nanny position."

Whitney let go of her hair, took a cigarette from her purse, and raised an eyebrow at Zara. "A nanny with a dog like that? Around kids?"

Daniella smiled. "Zara is well trained. She follows directions better than most people." She pointed to the No Smoking sign.

Whitney's lips went white as she pressed them together, shoving the cigarette back in her purse. Her husband laughed. "She got you, honey."

Whitney stood, shoving her chair back. "Suddenly, I'm not hungry." She marched out, clutching her purse.

Matt sighed. "I guess I'm supposed to go smooth the troubled waters. Some honeymoon." He got up and trudged upstairs.

Super. Two upset guests before lunch was even served. Sam gestured Paul and Edward into their chairs. "Will Ingrid be joining us?"

"In a minute," Paul said. "Something about changing her blouse."

Sam gestured Daniella to join the guests. "Might as well enjoy one last peaceful meal before you take on a preschooler." Daniella took a seat, and Zara settled at her side.

"Does she go everywhere with you?" Edward asked.

"Yes," she said. "But only on days that end in *y*."

He laughed but darted a few more unsettled looks at the dog.

Sam eased back into the kitchen to give the guests some privacy. He seated Oliver at the small table with a plate of food. "Gotta eat the salad too, son, not just the bread and butter."

After a few minutes, Sam peeked into the dining room again, checked on what needed to be refreshed or refilled. Daniella was sipping from a glass of ice water, Zara calm and relaxed. The serious cop was lovely, he thought, watching her dark eyes taking in every bit of chatter from the guests. Lovely? He grabbed a dish towel and began rubbing the already clean counter. He was reaching for a bottle of vinegar spray when a crash split the air.

Upstairs.

Sam was in motion immediately, but Daniella and Zara beat him to the stairwell.

He raced up behind her, taking the steps two at a time, almost slamming into Whitney, who was running down the stairs with Ingrid right behind her.

"What's wrong?" Daniella demanded.

Zara was stiff-legged, ears pricked.

"Something in the library," Whitney panted. "I was walking past, and Ingrid bolted out and almost knocked me over."

Ingrid sighed and fluttered her hands. "Sorry. I panicked." She looked at Sam. "And I knocked into the shelf. I think I might have broken something."

Sam urged the women a few paces away from the library door. "What scared you?"

Matt poked his head out of his bedroom. "Oh, there you are, Whit. What's going on? I heard a crash."

Daniella started to issue a command, but Sam spoke over her in a gentler tone.

"Nothing serious. Something fell and broke in the library."

Daniella closed her mouth and stepped aside to allow Sam to move in front of her. They entered the small space that had been intended to be a utility room before Hannah had insisted they convert it into a reading nook, complete with repurposed bookshelves and an old card catalog cabinet converted for storage and display. Before he crossed the threshold, Daniella regained the lead.

"Wait," she whispered to him.

She and Zara went inside first. He gave her a minute's head start before he entered, jaw tight. She was the cop, but it was his lodge.

The heat pouring in from the open window hit him immediately. His foot crunched against something. Looking down, he found the remnants of a clay horse on the floor.

"Look," Daniella said.

Sam thought at first she was talking to him, until he watched Zara lope around the room, sniffing. She applied her quivering nose behind the overstuffed chair, under the curtains and in the darkened alcove before she circled back to Daniella's feet.

"No one here," Daniella said, moving to the window. "Did you leave this open?"

"No way. We pay too much for the air-conditioning." He poked his head into the hallway to find Whitney, who'd joined Matt staring from their bedroom. With everything safe, he gestured for the women to rejoin them.

Ingrid and Whitney looked into the library. Matt

scooted close too, actively listening in. Sam couldn't exactly blame him for his curiosity.

Daniella's need to ask questions was emanating off her in waves, but she had to play the part of the nanny, so it was up to him.

"What happened exactly?" Sam said.

Ingrid grimaced. "I was looking for a book. It was hot, so I was trying to make it snappy. A bird flew in the window and scared me. I backed up into this shelf and broke the horse before I bolted out the door and into Whitney. I'm sorry."

"No need to be sorry," he said, though his heart squeezed a little at the broken bits of clay.

Ingrid watched as he picked up the ruined horse. "It was Hannah's, wasn't it?" she said, putting a hand on his forearm. "I remember she loved to collect things. And she spoke often about the lodge where she'd spent so much time." She sighed. "She said when the new lodge was built, she'd make sure to have enough room for her collections."

"Yes," he said. They'd laughed over the number of boxes she'd filled when they'd prepared to move into the lodge. "Hannah loved her treasures."

Daniella scanned the rough-beamed ceiling. "No birds now."

Ingrid wrapped her arms at her narrow shoulders. "That's a relief. It flew out, I think. Sorry I screamed." She grimaced. "Did I hurt you when I plowed into you, Whitney?"

She grinned. "Nah. I have three brothers. I know how to fend off a tackle. But you were running, so I figured something scary was coming and I also ran."

She shivered. "I would have been scared with some bird flying at me too."

Ingrid sighed. "I'm so sorry I broke the horse, Sam."

"Don't blame yourself," Sam said. "The window should never have been left open." *And it wasn't.*

"I thought it was odd to have it open when it's still so hot outside," Ingrid said. "I figured I'd tell you when I went downstairs."

"Yeah." Sam caught Daniella looking at him. "Must have been an oversight."

Edward and Paul edged in behind the women. Mae topped the staircase, Oliver on her hip, holding his new triceratops. She glanced past the group to the broken horse. "Uh-oh. Let's go get the broom, Oliver."

"Now that we've got this cleared up, does this mean we can eat?" Edward said. "Wouldn't want that lunch to get stale. It smells fantastic."

"Of course," Sam said. "I'll shut the window while you all head to the dining room."

When the guests had left, Daniella arched a brow at him. "Unlocked?"

He nodded. "The latch is broken, so it never did secure properly. It completely slipped my mind that it needed repair. Do you think someone climbed up the drainpipe from outside and into the library?"

"Possibly."

"Why would they bother? There's nothing in here but old books and some knickknacks."

"Any of the knickknacks valuable?"

"Some might get a few bucks at a flea market, but mostly the value is sentimental."

Daniella considered. "Ingrid might have been lying.

Maybe she opened the window and made up the bird story."

"Again...why would she?"

Daniella looked around. "Is anything missing?"

Sam pulled the love seat away from the wall and opened the glass doors of the display cabinet and double-checked. "Doesn't seem to be. Three snow globes, none worth much and all still accounted for. Maybe a book might be gone from the shelf, but that's what's supposed to be missing from a library."

"Old books? Worth anything?"

"My wife's from college and some we collected along the way. I'm a big reader, travelogues and such, most of them secondhand. No first editions. We had one of those, but we sold it."

Daniella reached down to stroke Zara's fur. There was something thoughtful in the cop's expression.

"Care to share your thoughts?" he said.

Daniella paused. "Not just yet. Let's go down to meet the others."

He bridled. Did she think him too much of a civilian? "If it means anything, I was an ordnance officer in the army for five years. I can handle tough scenarios, and I can keep my mouth shut. Besides, this is my place."

Instead of hostility, a smile curved her lips that softened her face altogether. It made his heart thunk for some reason. "All right. Here's where my mind went. The two women and Matt and Paul were not with us when you brought out the meal."

He nodded. "Which gave any of them time to sneak in here, even climb up the drainpipe and open the window."

"If that's what happened."

"And if that's *how* it happened," he added. "Really unlikely if you ask me. And why would any of the guests bother with something that elaborate when they all had easy access to the upstairs?"

"Unless they were hoping to sneak in unseen while everyone else was eating lunch."

Sam shook his head. "Makes no sense at all to me."

"More questions than answers," Daniella said. "That's why I love police work. One bunny trail leads to another until you eventually find the path."

"I can't wait for 'eventually.' I'm worried about my livelihood and my son."

"I didn't mean to trivialize it." She paused, the warmth dissolving from her expression in favor of the no-nonsense look. "Sam, I have to ask, so don't get offended. Are you sure you shut the window?"

He was careful to keep the irritation from his voice. "Yes, ma'am. I shut the window. No question." *I'm not a fool.*

Did she believe him? Not knowing her well, he'd guess she did. He didn't have to utter his next question because he saw the same one nestled in the gleaming ebony of her eyes.

Then what had just happened?

And why?

THREE

He picked up the keys and headed to the old building. Oliver was in his room for his post lunch nap while Mae, within easy earshot, changed the sheets in the guest rooms. What would he do without Mae? She was a straight-up gift from God. She enjoyed the money earned from her duties, saving for that elusive trip to the tropics that she constantly talked about. His other part-time employee, John Payat, had taken the guests to Silver City, the sunny hilltop town where they would tour Fort Bayard and the City of Rocks State Park. Sam was relieved to have them off the property for a few hours.

Daniella and Zara both eyed him as he passed through the courtyard. The tilt of their heads was identical. He chuckled.

"Don't worry, Zara. I'm not going farther than the old inn," he said.

Zara snaked her tail back and forth. Daniella offered that polite smile he figured was her "on duty" look. He wondered about her real personality, the one hidden behind the badge. The glimpses into the complicated woman he'd seen intrigued him and that, in turn, awakened both guilt and interest. He noticed a pendant hanging on a chain around her neck, gold with a mark on it he couldn't see clearly.

She caught his gaze and hastily tucked it beneath her collar.

Message received. *She's not here to share, Sam.* She's got a job to do. *Why don't you stick to yours?*

"I checked the outbuildings this morning," she said. "No sign of anything tampered with or windows left open."

Left open? He was about to quibble when he shook it off. She was doing her job. He should do his. Business, remember? "All right. Thank you."

She paused and jutted her chin toward the sunlit adobe walls of the Cliffside. "I like the architecture, the way the new lodge mirrors the old."

She'd noticed that? He hoped his wide grin wasn't too big for the size of the compliment. "Thank you. The old lodge had been in Hannah's family for generations, and she had so many memories attached to it. We didn't want to discard the past, just take inspiration from it, so we kept the old lodge intact and built the new one from the ground up." Countless hours he and Hannah had spent tweaking and reworking the plans. They'd drawn and sketched their dream lodge using everything from computer models to crayons. Bittersweet memories.

She arched an eyebrow as she took in the rich plantings surrounding them in the courtyard and the cliffs beyond. Tipping her face to the sun, she said, "'Behold, I will do a new thing; now it shall spring forth; shall ye not know it? I will even make a way in the wilderness, and rivers in the desert.'"

Zara let out a yip.

He gaped. Never would he have expected Daniella to recite scripture.

She laughed. "Surprised? I noticed you have a Bible in every room, so I figured we have something in common on the subject. Zara waits for me to read a passage every night. That means it's lights out." Daniella looked at Zara. "Sorry, girl. That was just a bonus passage today. Not bedtime yet."

He wasn't quite sure what to say, but he found himself delighting in this new facet of the tough cop.

Daniella peeked at her phone, brows crimping into that "I'm on duty" look. "Sorry, but I have to get online for a meeting."

"Yes, ma'am."

"And you don't have to call me ma'am," she said, attention fixed on the laptop. He almost missed the second part as he turned to go. "Her Royal Eminence will do."

He was still chuckling over that one as he strolled away and opened the door to the original lodge.

The perfume of age and memories washed over him. He would never forget that this had been Hannah's family cabin, the spot she'd spent holidays and summers, basking in the sizzling heat to which she'd always seemed immune. He'd visited once too, after their engagement, and promptly fallen in love with the creaky place. Now it was used exclusively for storage and clerical duties because he could not bear to have it knocked down. Across the courtyard, the new lodge gleamed golden; the old and the new. The beauty of it struck him afresh. A way in the wilderness, indeed.

We did good, Hannah. Oliver has an amazing place to live.

If only the boy had his mother to share it with. Embracing the new meant leaving the past behind, and how could he do that without allowing Oliver's mother to disappear from his life? It was the central question that plagued him daily.

From the living room window, he watched Daniella settle in the shade of a carefully pruned pinyon, waiting for what looked to be a serious conference call. He'd gotten the sense that whatever was brewing back at headquarters was the case Daniella yearned to be in on. Her real work, not some babysitting job for him and Oliver. But she was tough and professional, a cop's cop, and she'd do her best.

As he watched, she bent and kissed Zara's nose so tenderly it awakened an ache in his chest. She tossed the ball and the dog raced to pounce on it, a blur of churning legs, while she logged on to her computer. He wanted to stay there and watch her, to see the casual interaction of this anything-but-casual woman who knew scripture and didn't trust him to close the windows properly. What a muddle.

Get moving, his gut urged. There was always a mountain of tasks to accomplish each day, and he tried to maximize the moments during Oliver's nap. The linens he was looking for this time were in the hall closet, egg-yolk yellow with intricate embroidery. He had to move a box of antique silver to get to them. He stopped, mid movement. Hadn't he put the silver on the bottom shelf after he'd used the pieces for an extravagant Fourth of July spread?

He stood there, staring at the box, struggling to remember. Had someone moved it, or was it his own forgetfulness borne of attention deficit? He was still trying to process what he'd learned about himself only recently. It had hit him when he'd been reading a parenting book, borrowed from the library. Attention deficit... all the hallmarks applied to him, though it had been assumed he was merely a poor student with impulse control problems. Maybe that's why he'd gravitated to bomb disposal in the military. It required a one-hundred-percent concentration level that left no room for distraction. In the civilian world, he struggled to keep his thoughts from running off in all directions.

He sighed. Whatever the label, he often zoomed from thing to thing without finishing, and forgot way more than he should unless he left notes for himself on his phone. It had only worsened since Hannah died. Was that the case with the silver? Maybe he'd stowed the box on a different shelf? Sounded just like something he'd do.

Or left a window open? he thought grimly. That was certainly a simpler explanation for what had happened the night before than some sort of conspiracy. He had been fiddling with that window recently, trying to air out the smell of some touch-up paint. What if it was nothing more than his poor memory working against him? The thought made him heat up with shame. "Move it, Kavanaugh," he ordered himself.

Sliding the box back into its proper place, he grabbed the linens. He'd promised Mae to snag the aged family cookbook that had a recipe for homemade pickles she wanted to try. Sam had learned to accept sharing some cooking duties with Mae, since she loved banging around the stove as much as he did. Still, he considered it his territory, like he always had. Hannah had been the decorating genius and guest coordinator, but the cooking duties had always been his. He was proud that he'd demonstrated to Oliver how to make toast and pancakes, so far. Next stop, scrambled eggs. Oliver would be a competent cook when he was old enough.

The cookbooks were crammed into a tiny cupboard

next to the ancient refrigerator, which he suspected would probably stay in service long after the sleek stainless-steel model in the lodge went to its final reward. He slid open the front window to catch any hint of breeze since the old place had no air-conditioning. Daniella somehow heard the movement of the creaking window and turned to wiggle her fingers at him before she clicked a button on her computer.

Another disconcerting juxtaposition of the familiar and the formal. How should he be feeling about Daniella? Certainly, he shouldn't be thinking about her as much as he was, but it would be strange to have any woman on the grounds, attentive to him and Oliver, cop or not. Usually, Sam was able to be anonymous, the genial host who facilitated rather than interacted on a deep level. Daniella upset the equilibrium he'd fought so hard to attain.

Unusual circumstances, he told himself. Everything would return to normal as soon as they figured out what was going on. Thoughts scrolled through his mind as he found the cookbook and selected fat golden candles to add to the table. The open window, broken bits of Hannah's horse...

As Daniella had observed, Ingrid, Whitney, Matt and Paul were not downstairs the whole time. Any of them might have arranged for the open window for some nefarious purpose. Did that mean Edward, who'd not left the dining room, was clear of any involvement? Not really. The man could have climbed up and pried open the window earlier and searched the library, if that was his intent, though it still seemed ridiculous when all the guests had easy access via the stairs. Or maybe Sam *had* left the window open himself. Where did all these mental gymnastics get him?

Down another rabbit trail, as Daniella would have said. He couldn't share her enthusiasm for the chase. To him, it was about his life and his son's. He turned his mind to the brisket he needed to marinate for dinner. Gathering the fresh herbs from the courtyard garden was the next thing on the to-do list. Letting himself out, he balanced the borrowed items on one hip and palmed the bunch of keys to lock the front door.

They felt strange, lighter than they should have, something he'd not noticed when he'd grabbed them from the hook in the lodge kitchen. He held them up and peered. Old lodge key. New lodge key. Others for the shed, SUV, gate. And one he didn't know what it unlocked. His breath stopped. Where was the master key? The one that unlocked all the doors in the main lodge, a failsafe since the bedroom doors were not equipped with fancy card readers. *We can't have card entry locks at the Cliffside*, Hannah had insisted. *It ruins the whole feel of the place.* Old-fashioned bolts were the only security, and the master key that unlocked all of them was missing.

His thoughts tripped one over the other.

What if the open window had been meant as a distraction? With the air-conditioning on, a guest would likely notice and bring it to his attention. That would put him into action, leaving somebody a moment to slip into the kitchen and remove the master key.

His panicked brain filled in the rest.

If the master had been taken, then someone had access to the house...to Oliver.

"I wish we had more to report," RMK9 Unit Sergeant Tyson Wilkes said to the officers in the video conference. The lines of fatigue grooving his forehead indicated the Baby Chloe case was clearly wearing on him. "We've still got a missing baby and not much in the way of leads. Good news is Kate Montgomery is showing signs of consciousness."

Daniella straightened in her excitement. The unresponsive woman found near the torched car—and the pink baby blanket and infant car seat—was their only potential witness thus far. "Did she say anything?"

"Not yet," Officer Reece Campbell put in. His German shepherd, Maverick, poked his nose into the camera view for a moment. "But when she does, we'll be there."

Daniella resisted the urge to smack her hand on her thigh. *If she does...* Her own cynicism worried her. It was part of the reason she'd been wondering lately if law enforcement was her future. She was good at it, no question, and she loved her work and Zara, but she'd had a feeling of restlessness recently that she couldn't will away, a sense that she wasn't supposed to be a cop forever.

FBI Special Agent in Charge Michael Bridges cleared his throat. He was the big boss, to whom Tyson reported. Daniella caught the slight rigidity in Tyson's shoulders. Since one of their K-9s Shadow, had been injured in a freak accident, during a training session and later several dogs had mysteriously gotten out of their enclosures, Michael had made noises that brought Tyson's leadership into question, which did not bode well for the unit. The RMK9 Unit was relatively new and on probationary status for a year to determine its need. Michael was doing his job, but Daniella wished he'd butt out and let them do theirs.

"We're aware of a baby smuggling ring operating in the western states," Michael said. "Could be Chloe Baker is a victim."

Baby smuggling. A murdered mother. A hospital-
ized witness. Daniella felt a physical tug. Surely those
cases would be more suitable for her skills than where
she now found herself. But she could not deny the instincts telling her that something was seriously wrong
at the lodge. She clicked off her musings when Tyson
asked her for an update.

"I'm installing security cameras as soon as I can get
them," she said.

"So you're convinced there's a threat?"

"Not certain, but there's a whole lot of weirdness
surrounding this place."

"How's the nanny cover working out?" Officer Chris
Fuller asked, a sardonic lift to his brow.

She resisted the urge to roll her eyes. "Oliver is
adorbs, but I'm finding it hard to remember to play the
part. Mary Poppins, I'm not."

"You'll get the hang of it." Ben Sawyer, the other protection dog handler in the unit and a new father, gave
her a thumbs-up. "I can now change a diaper without
even gagging. And those midnight bottles are no sweat."

"Thanks, but we're past the diaper and bottle stage
with Oliver, fortunately," she said with a smile, ignoring the twinge she always felt when the topic of babies
came up.

"Keep us posted," Tyson said.

After a few more minutes of wrap-up and more unsolicited childcare tips, the call ended.

Nanny. The cover was more of a burden than a benefit. How exactly was she going to get to the bottom
of the threat and appear to tend to a three-year-old?
That was more frightening than any other case she'd
attempted. But she didn't actually have to care for him,

right? Just pretend to do so for a few days until she shed some light on the case. No problem.

"How hard can it be to manage a preschooler?" she said to Zara. The dog scrambled up and dropped the ball in Daniella's lap. He cocked his head as if to say, "Remember when I was in training as a puppy and ate a hole in my crate and chewed your computer printer into little pieces?"

Fortunately, human children didn't have the same intensity as Malinois puppies. Dogs, particularly Zara's mouthy, frenetic breed, needed to be constantly busy. Maybe it worked the same for children.

Suddenly, Zara's playful mood vanished. She sat up and yipped as Sam ran up the path, long legs churning.

Daniella leaped to her feet as Sam skidded to a stop. The fear sizzled on his face like a live wire. "The master key is missing from my keyring. I think the open window was a diversion to get me out of the kitchen so someone could steal it."

"Where's Oliver?"

"In the house, napping. Mae's there but I tried calling and texting. She isn't answering her phone."

They sprinted the remaining distance together, but Zara outpaced them both. Daniella put her in a sit to allow Sam to open the door. To his credit, his hands did not tremble. The soldier in him, probably.

"Mae," he shouted as they plunged inside. Daniella didn't hear a response, but Zara clearly did. She barked and Daniella gave her the command to follow her instincts. The dog bounded toward the kitchen.

"Can you find Mae?" Sam turned to the stairwell. "I'm going to Oliver."

Daniella nodded, in pursuit of her canine partner.

The dog skidded across the tile in her haste to get to a small corner door. It led to the basement. Daniella had examined the space the night before, a neatly ordered storage area with wall-to-wall shelves and tidily stacked boxes of pantry staples. Zara barked and clawed at the wood. The brass latch had been activated, locking whomever it was inside.

"Help," a muffled voice cried.

Daniella ordered Zara off and undid the latch. Mae almost tumbled into Daniella's waiting arms, breathing hard.

"What happened?" Daniella demanded.

Mae shook her head so hard it sent her white hair flying. "I'm not sure. I was getting some paper towels and I heard the latch flip," she panted, bent over. "I couldn't imagine who would have done it, since we've never locked the door, to my knowledge. I hollered and ran up the stairs, figuring it was Sam or something, but no one came to free me. I didn't have my phone so I couldn't call for help. I've been yelling for fifteen minutes."

Fifteen minutes. A long time for someone to have free rein of the house. Her stomach tightened. Had Sam found Oliver?

"Are you injured?" Daniella asked.

"No." Mae pressed a hand to her chest. "Winded is all. I'll just sit down here for a minute and catch my breath."

Daniella was already running, Zara at her heels. They pounded up the stairs and down the end of the hall, almost colliding with Sam as he plunged out.

His face was stark, eyes glittering feverishly. She knew before he said a word.

"He's not here," Sam said, terror thickening his voice to a low baritone. "Oliver's gone!"

FOUR

Sam snatched up the plastic dinosaur that lay on the floor, looking frantically in all directions. He ran to the bed and peered underneath, but Daniella had already discounted that possible hiding place as well as the closet because Zara would have known instantly if the boy, or anyone else, had been concealed there.

"Zara, find," Daniella said. Before she finished the command, the dog was already sprinting out of the room and into the hallway.

Daniella knew Sam was in agony, wondering if Oliver had been abducted, hurt, or worse. Agony was not a luxury allowed to an on-duty cop. Still, her own heart thumped irregularly as she ran after Zara to the back stairwell. The dog's nose was glued to the floor as she galloped. Oliver was so young, innocent. That ache hit her in the small vulnerable place where she bottled up thoughts of another child she'd lost twelve years before. Her own. A fragile perfect newborn. Thrusting those thoughts away, she ran on. *Just find him. Get him back to his dad.* Zara raced along with Daniella in pursuit, Sam two steps behind.

The dog slammed into the panic bar at the stairwell

door, her fifty-five pounds of muscle flinging it wide. Nothing could stand between the determined Malinois and her objective. Sunlight momentarily dazzled Daniella's eyes as they exited the building, so she heard rather than saw a childish squeal that drew her like a magnet.

Oliver.

Daniella barreled into the sizzling sunlight, stumbling until her vision gradually cleared.

Joy danced through her senses. Zara was in a barely contained sit next to Oliver. The boy was wrapped in his blanket, sitting in the shade of an enormous fir tree fifty yards from the exit door. His face was puffy and wet with tears, but he did not appear to be hurt.

Sam rushed past her and bundled his boy into a tight hug. "Thank You, God," he said over and over, and the emotion in his voice made something in Daniella's chest tighten again.

Yes, she agreed. *Thank You, God.*

"Zara," she said, calling the dog to her, "let's give them a moment." She pulled a small squishy ball from her pocket and tossed it to Zara to reward her. "Good girl," she said as the dog scrambled to retrieve it. "You get to sleep with Nettie tonight." She turned to Sam. "I'm going back inside to clear the building."

He managed a nod, his chest still heaving as he clutched his son. She laid her hand on his shoulder for a moment, hoping he could feel her own relief and reassurance. His muscles quivered under her touch. With a confident nod, she left them.

It was unlikely whoever had locked Mae in the basement was nearby or Zara would have remained tense, but the dog might have been distracted following Oliver. Daniella had never known Zara to overlook an important detail, but there was too much at stake to risk it.

Zara remained calm as they approached the inn, returning through the back door and retracing their steps to Oliver's bedroom, the hallway, and a quick sweep of the upper floors. Nothing looked amiss, but she would need Sam to confirm. They did another sweep of the main floor and headed back to the kitchen. No sign of an intruder.

Someone had locked Mae downstairs. But why take Oliver only to put him outside in the yard alone? Who could it have been and where had they gone? All the guests were supposedly in Silver City, but that didn't mean one of them hadn't rerouted and returned by taxi or Uber.

Mae sat in the kitchen, fingers knitted together. She grabbed the edge of the table when she saw Zara. "I heard running," Mae said. "Where's Sam? Has he got Oliver? Please tell me Oliver isn't hurt."

"They're both okay." It occurred to Daniella that Mae could have been working with someone else who'd locked her in the basement as a diversion. But surely her panic had been authentic? The worry on her face communicating her love and fear? Assumptions got people killed, she reminded herself. Mae would have to be checked out, like everyone else on the property. "I'll be back in a few minutes." She and Zara headed for the rear door on the way outside to Sam when Mae cleared her throat meaningfully.

Daniella shot her a look. "Yes?"

"If you don't mind me saying so, you don't act much like a nanny."

Daniella cringed inwardly. *I forgot to play the part.* She should be the one staying with the child while Sam checked the property. Busted. While she stood there, searching for a response, Mae smiled.

"I understand that sometimes, um, certain situations call for nannies with unusual skills," Mae said. She slid her eyes to Zara. "And trained dogs."

Daniella locked eyes with Mae. "Yes," she said slowly. "That's right."

Mae's smile disappeared. "I've worked here since Hannah and Sam built this place. It's been a struggle from day one. Just as they'd managed to get the lodge open, Hannah was diagnosed with cancer. I was there through the whole ordeal and, believe me, they both fought valiantly. I saw how Sam grieved his wife's death and I watch how he gives everything he has to this place and his son."

Daniella waited, breath held.

Mae paused, lifting her chin a little higher. "So I say, whatever needs to be done to protect Oliver and Sam is fine by me. They are good people and they really need a…um…special nanny right now."

Daniella considered the woman before her. To trust or not to trust? Her gut said yes, but she'd been wrong before and trust wasn't on her top ten list. Mae couldn't have locked herself in the basement, but she might have had an accomplice to allow for a distraction. Finally, she said, "It would be best if the guests didn't know my… special qualifications."

Mae nodded, mimed zipping her lips and tossing the key.

Daniella had no choice but to hope the woman was what she appeared to be. "Thank you." She jogged out with Zara to check the old inn before she returned to Sam. Oliver wasn't crying anymore, but he was hugging his dad tightly around the neck, his blanket wadded up under his chin.

"Hi, Oliver," Daniella said. He wiggled his small fingers at her in a half-hearted wave. The gesture made her go mushy inside. She cleared her throat. "Wasn't it neat the way Zara found you?" Was that a suitable thing to say to a terrified child? She flicked a look at Sam, but he was staring at his son.

Oliver nodded, and now she detected a sliver of a smile. Maybe she'd soothed him after all. It put a smile on her own face. Super Nanny indeed. "Can you tell me what happened? How did you get outside?"

Oliver hid his face in his father's chest.

He was terrified, but it had to be faced. "I know you're frightened, but talking about it will let some of the scary feelings out."

Oliver looked at her then and launched into a garbled story from which she could only snag a word or two. She turned helplessly to Sam.

"He told me some before you came," Sam said. "He said he heard a noise in the hallway. He opened the door to look. There was someone wearing a mask in the library. And he doesn't know if it was a man or woman. He got scared, so he ran away and used our emergency exit plan." Sam could not hide the pride. "We practiced the escape routes in case there's a fire or other problem." Sam pressed a fierce kiss to his son's temple. "I'm proud of you, Ollie. Mommy would be proud, too." Sam's voice broke as he said it.

Oliver didn't react at the mention of his mother. Instead his brow furrowed. "There's a bad man in there. I don't wanna go back."

Sam squeezed him close, his own expression pained. "I know you were scared, buddy, but…"

"But I'm here to be your nanny, remember?" Daniella interrupted brightly. "That means Zara and I are going to stay here with you so you won't be alone. How would that be?"

Oliver's countenance brightened immediately.

Sam's caramel eyes sought hers. "You'll stay until this is over? I thought maybe you were going to take off after the cameras were installed."

She regarded the big man cradling his small boy, and her stomach flipped. There was no way she would leave them vulnerable and alone. For a moment, she was captured by the gratitude in his demeanor, the strength. He was the kind of God-fearing, honest man that every child deserved. She blinked away her stupor. "Yep. Zara and I are taking the job, but we don't dust or do windows. Purely protection, got it?"

He chuckled. "Yes, ma'am." He hugged Oliver. "You can call her Nanny Daniella. Can you say that?"

"Nanny Ella," Oliver said gravely.

Daniella laughed. "Close enough."

"All right, Nanny Ella," Sam said. "What's our first move?"

"We go to town and pick up the security cameras, and while we're there maybe we can check on the guests. You know," she said darkly, "to make sure they have everything they need." And to count heads. The people who knew the most about the inn were those staying in it: Edward Reese, Paul and Ingrid Zariya, Whitney and Matt Poleman, Mae, and Sam's part-time guide John Payat, whom she had yet to meet. One of them was guilty. Of course it was possible it was an outside enemy from Sam or Hannah's past, but her gut told her otherwise. The danger was close, very close.

Sam put Oliver down and took him firmly by the hand. "We're going to Silver City, son."

She understood. There was no way he was leaving Oliver at the lodge with Mae. Fine, since she intended to be the most attentive nanny ever hired until she made the arrest.

And that arrest would come soon.

No doubt about it.

Sam drove the SUV down the mountain road toward Silver Springs. He turned on the music for Oliver, a snappy selection of preschool songs that earned him raised eyebrows from Daniella. Oliver was humming away and too distracted to listen to the grown-up conversation, he hoped. Good parenting, he figured, was mostly about deciding what to share with children and when.

His nerves were still zinging at the memory of his son being missing, even for only a few moments. Daniella mused aloud. "The searcher knew they wouldn't have much time. It could be a matter of minutes until you returned from the old lodge and found Mae locked in the basement. If she'd had her phone, it might have been less."

"Maybe not." He groaned. "If they'd been watching my routines, they'd know my schedule. During Oliver's nap time, I normally spend an hour at least taking care of business details on the old computer I have there. There's a phone I use to call in orders and such also. They'd probably assume they had a good sixty minutes before I came back and discovered Mae missing, especially if they'd seen her cell phone on the counter where she always leaves it. And they planned on Oliver staying asleep."

His mind wouldn't allow him to consider other ideas the intruder might have had to silence his son, should he have awakened. He swallowed a lump in his throat. At least he was vindicated about leaving the window open. "Somebody set up the whole open-window thing to give themselves a chance to steal the master key. Weird though. If they were after money, or trying to steal credit card info or something, they'd search my office in the old lodge, not the main house."

"They might not have realized your office space wasn't on the main property," Daniella said. "They weren't after your office information anyway. And I didn't see anything there worth stealing. No offense. Some petty cash, an older model computer that is password protected…" Her lip quirked. "And your impressive button collection. I did wonder what human could possibly require that many buttons in one lifetime."

He laughed. It felt strange and he realized he hadn't laughed with another grown-up in a long time. "My mother had this jar of buttons on her shelf for decades. She always said, 'You never know when you might need one.' The guys in my military unit always teased me for having a stash of buttons, but when they needed one, they sang a different tune. I find a lot of lost buttons in this business, so I just keep chucking them in."

He sighed. "Hannah laughed about it too." Including both Daniella and Hannah in the same conversation? Strange, for sure. He shrugged it off. "Anyway, nothing worth stealing, I agree. Frankly, aside from the furniture, I don't think there's much worth swiping in the new lodge, either. We have art and décor, sure, but nothing priceless. We don't even have a big-screen TV in either lodge."

"I've cataloged some handmade pottery and a collection of paintings. What about that?"

He shot a look in the rearview at Oliver, who was stroking Zara behind the ears, lost in the music. "Hannah spent summers here throughout her life and she loved collecting things. Even when she was in college in Germany, she displayed some of her pieces there to remind her of home. When she passed…" Another quick look at Oliver. "Hannah's mom insisted on having all of the collectibles appraised. She figured we might be able to sell some to start a college fund for Oliver." He shrugged. "Nothing there valued more than five hundred dollars. I did sell one piece, an antique basket, and opened a savings account for Oliver, but nothing else was worth selling." In truth, he couldn't stand to part with any of it anyway. Each object was a memory; a tangible way to tell Oliver about his mother. Letting go heaped pain upon pain.

"I've known people to steal for less than that, but I agree that whoever is behind this is taking huge risks, too huge for a simple petty theft."

"The locks," Sam said suddenly. "I'll have to change them all." His pulse ratcheted up a notch. "Don't have the money right now," he said, his cheeks warming at the admission. He probably shouldn't have said it out loud, but Daniella's forthright attitude made him want to reciprocate.

"Start with Oliver's room," she said, "and the front door locks for the new and old lodge. You can replace the others gradually or hey, even better, maybe we solve this thing and you don't have to replace them at all." She shot him a cheeky grin.

"You're a nanny of many talents."

She waved an airy hand. "Mary Poppins has nothing on me." Her smile was a mixture of cockiness, sympathy and dedication.

He found himself grinning back. Though the clench in his stomach of finding Oliver missing was still there, Daniella's presence eased his mind. He found he could even engage in chitchat as they drove along about their shared enthusiasm for hockey, the outdoors, her interest in rappelling. Chitchat…with another woman? He banished the sliver of guilt. This was more of a business partnership than a friendship. No harm in that, was there? She did not seem to mind his frequent changes in topic.

"You love this area don't you?" Daniella asked after he enthused about the great places to rock climb around Silver City.

He sighed. "Yeah. Wish I could spend more time exploring."

"I love being outside. I feel the wide-open spaces calling to me more and more. When I give up the cop gig, I'm considering working for the national park servic or running a guide business."

He raised an eyebrow. "Quit the force? I would have pegged you for a lifer."

She huffed. "Why? Because I appear to have no interests outside of law enforcement?"

He could not tell by her flat tone if he'd offended. "No…uh, just your commitment to the job, is all."

"I love being a cop, but Zara has the beginnings of arthritis and she's going to have to retire soon. And it wears on me, all the paperwork and red tape, being in the office and such. All the cases where I was too late to make a difference stick in my mind." She shrugged.

"Feel like I'm missing out on something else I'm supposed to be doing."

"I hear you. I keep worrying that running the lodge prevents me from properly exposing Oliver to the natural wonders around here. Gobbles up the daddy-and-son moments we're supposed to be having. Lodge duties expand to suck up all the available time, no matter how late I work or early I get up." He shook his head. "Dunno when I started to become a worrier. Never was that kind before. My army buddies used to call me Captain Sunshine," he said. "That was a lifetime ago." Before Oliver. Before cancer. Before assuming sole ownership of a lodge that consumed every waking moment. Why was it all fountaining from his mouth? Delayed shock?

She took in the brush-covered earth, silent for a moment. "I've heard raising kids is kind of like having your heart walking around outside your body."

There was something pensive in her tone and still she did not quite look at him. Daniella had a secret. That much was clear. "Are you...do you have kids?"

She cocked an eyebrow at him. "Kind of a personal question."

Flushing, he cleared his throat. "Oh. Sorry. Didn't mean to pry."

"It's fair. You've let me in on your life." Gazing out the window, she finally answered. "I'm not a parent."

Not a parent, but something had triggered emotion in the stoic cop. *Not your business, Sam.* He decided to try some tact for a change. "Well, in my experience, there's a million ways to fail at parenting. Guess that's why there are so many books on the subject. I've probably read them all."

She looked at Oliver in the back seat, silent for a hair

too long. "You're making a life for him filled with unconditional love. That's not a fail."

And it made him feel better to hear it. "Did you, uh, did you have parents like that? Or maybe that's too personal, too? Sorry again. I'm out of practice talking to people other than guests."

She flashed him an indecipherable look. "It's okay. My mom was an alcoholic and Dad abandoned my brother Rico and me when we were kids. Rico is five years older and landed in a good foster situation. Mine wasn't that great, but I survived it, and it made me tough. I met a man who saved my life. I call him Uncle Cal, biology notwithstanding." Her smile was soft then. "Love doesn't have to be biological. That's a lesson I learned the hard way."

Again she showed that strange distant look, as if she was peering inside herself.

"That was a lot to deal with as a child," he said. "You're a strong person." Confusing and comforting at the same time, this woman. He was relieved when they entered Silver City. The town of ten thousand people boasted a historic district and some trendy eateries to accommodate locals and the increasing tourist revenue from those seeking to experience the Gila Wilderness. In his view, it was the perfect spot for travelers looking to get away from it all yet still enjoy great food, funky boutiques and other amenities.

"Find the guests first or hit the hardware store?" he asked.

Daniella consulted her notes. "According to your itinerary, you arranged for them to have a snack and cold drink at the Buckhorn Opera House and stay for a show. It's almost curtain time. Easy way to count heads."

Nodding, he drove them up the mountaintop to the squat adobe building.

"How old is this place?" she said after a whistle.

"Built in 1860 after gold was discovered in the Pinos Altos Mountain."

"It looks it," she said, her arm on the door handle. "I'll take a quick peek inside."

"Hang on." He shook his head. "What reason exactly would a nanny have for popping into the opera house with her dog, all by her lonesome?"

She rolled her eyes. "My day off?"

"Not buying it."

Daniella sighed. "Got any better ideas, 'cuz you and Oliver aren't going in there alone."

"It just so happens that I do," he shot back. "I check on the guest activities from time to time. Why not today?"

"Lead on, Captain Sunshine."

"Shouldn't have divulged my embarrassing nickname."

She grinned. "Yeah, I'm going to get plenty of mileage out of that one."

Afternoon heat slammed them the moment they opened the vehicle doors. He unstrapped Oliver while she freed Zara. The sun was relentless, the reason he'd arranged for the opera stop, which allowed his guests to escape the peak heat hours. He'd never thought it would also provide an efficient way to spy on them. It went against his grain to poke into people's business, until he remembered the sensation of finding his son missing. One of his guests or someone else close to the lodge had terrified his son.

Nothing was going to keep him from finding out who was responsible.

Nothing, and no one.

FIVE

Daniella followed Sam, who took Oliver by the hand. Zara was eager to escort them inside, but Daniella put her into a sit in a subtle corner of the cool, covered porch. She'd bark if anyone approached her, and Daniella would be there in a moment. It was the only solution she could think of as the SUV would become deadly hot in a matter of moments, and Zara couldn't be seen with her "police dog" harness, which would have allowed her access to the building. The nanny disguise was proving a challenge in more ways than one.

The interior of the opera house was blessedly cool, scented by the aroma of fried onions that drifted from the dining room. Sam headed for the music, a cheerful show tune emanating from the stage where a Western-clad singer belted out a song backed by a guitarist, drummer and trumpet player. The interior was dark except for the old-timey chandeliers hanging overhead. Daniella allowed her eyes to adjust until she could just make out the rows of patrons sitting in chairs facing the stage. Maximum fifty people. Seats were probably first come, first serve, but there was a good chance

Sam's guests were clustered together since they'd traveled as a group.

Sam hoisted Oliver and began to scan the back rows. She went the other way, sidling along the outer aisle and working her way in. The dim light made the search harder. Someone bumped her elbow.

Edward Reese blinked at her in surprise. "Daniella?" he whispered. "What are you doing here?"

He was standing close enough that she felt the warmth of his body. He'd been sweating. Returning from outside? "Sam wanted to check in on the guests, so we came along for company," she whispered back. "Why aren't you watching the show?"

He lifted a shoulder. "Needed some air."

"Kinda hot to be outside."

"Not for me. I grew up in Texas. Concerts aren't my thing."

Nor hers either. Too crowded. "Where are you seated?"

He pointed to the back row, left side. Before she could ask about the others, he gave her a wave goodbye and squeezed through the row to take his seat. Sam had noticed her conversation and eased nearer. Together they counted heads.

Edward Reese sat next to newlywed Matthew, who appeared to be asleep with his chin on his chest. All the other chairs in the row were occupied by strangers. There was no sign of Whitney, Ingrid or her brother Paul.

They tiptoed back outside and rejoined Zara on the porch.

"We're two for five," Sam said.

"Maybe one for five." She told him what she'd observed about Edward. "He could have been returning from the lodge."

Sam frowned as a van pulled up with Cliffside Lodge on the side. A short, dark-haired man climbed out, brow furrowed.

"John," Sam called.

The man came over but stayed a few feet away, eyeing Zara. "I don't get paid to be your taxi service, Sam."

"Daniella, this is John Payat. He drives the guests for me and leads tours when the timing works for us both." He stared at John. "What's wrong?"

John took off his baseball cap and scrubbed his puff of hair away from his sweaty brow. "I dropped your guests for their mine tour and, after I picked them up to bring them here two hours ago, just like you told me, the ladies decided they'd rather visit the historic downtown." He balled a fist on his hip. "I had to schlep them there while the others stayed to watch the show. I'm supposed to snag everyone and take 'em to the lodge after the show, but now I gotta make another stop to retrieve the other two from downtown."

"Only the women?"

"Yeah."

"Not a man too? Paul Zariya?"

"Nah. I'm telling you, just the ladies. Next time, you're paying me more or you can drive 'em yourself."

Sam was about to reply when Daniella cut him off.

"That must be really annoying," she said to John. "Being treated like a driver at their beck and call."

John's shoulders relaxed a fraction. "You got that right."

"A waste of time when you could be doing something else," Daniella added.

"Exactly. Leaves me with a couple hours to kill but not enough to go home. What am I supposed to do? Already had my lunch in town. Wound up taking a nap in the van 'cuz there wasn't time to do much else."

"I missed lunch," Daniella said. "Where'd you go around here that's good?"

He jerked a thumb. "Good Mexican place down on Silver Heights Boulevard with a carne asada burrito on special today. Tasty and cheap. Got a kick to it 'cuz they know their way around jalapeños."

"Sounds fantastic."

"We're going into town right now," Sam said. "I'll pay for an Uber and have the women dropped here, okay? That should save you a trip."

"If you can find 'em," John grumbled. "They are slippery. Gonna get another quick nap." He looked at Danielle and quirked the smallest of smiles. "Let me know how you like the burrito."

They got back into the SUV, which was already sweltering.

Sam cranked the air conditioner. "That burrito business was a way of checking out John's story, wasn't it?"

"He had enough time to get back to the lodge. Give me a minute." She did a quick internet search on her phone. "He was right, that is the special at the burrito place. Doesn't clear him completely though. He's been around long enough to have memorized the weekly offerings."

Sam gaped, and she warmed at the flat-out admiration.

"Simple cop work," she said with a shrug.

"Not simple at all." He frowned. "But we've still got three unaccounted for—the two women and Paul.

Plus, John's story and Edward Reese's need checking because they both could have gone back to the lodge. What next?"

"We stop at the hardware store and get back to home base. I want to have the cameras installed before the guests return. If I'm clever with the placement, they might not notice for a while and we can get some intel."

"Oh, you're more than clever," Sam said. "You're a whiz."

"You can tell my boss." For a moment, she wondered why Sam's praise felt so good, way better than anything she'd received from her evaluations. "Anyway, let's get going because I don't know how much more preschool counting music I can take."

The selection wasn't great at the hardware store, but she was able to score three battery-powered cameras. They would have to do until she could get better ones. She'd also purchased a baby monitor with video capability, which Sam had instructed her to call a "walkie-talkie" instead of anything attached to "baby."

"Oliver doesn't like being called a baby," Sam explained.

Another thing she'd learned about preschoolers. They had independent streaks. Good for them. By the time she was five, she'd learned how to cook her own food and snitch cookies from the apartment lobby where she'd lived for a short time. Independence was a good thing.

But it's okay to need people too, Uncle Cal had finally taught her. That was a lesson she hadn't had much occasion to practice outside of work.

Back in the SUV, they cruised the downtown for fifteen minutes before they spotted Ingrid and Whitney exiting a gift shop along the historic main drag. For two women who'd never met before, they seemed very chummy. Daniella could count her girlfriends on one hand, namely Jodie Chen, Tyson's assistant. But maybe other women behaved more like Whitney and Ingrid? Bonding quickly and easily?

Or maybe they didn't. Was it possible that Whitney and Ingrid knew each other before they'd come to the lodge? Partners in the attack on Sam and terrorizing Oliver? Why, was the big question. She made a mental note to ask Jodie for some research help as Sam pulled the SUV to the curb and called to them.

The ladies stopped in surprise. Whitney pulled on a pair of oversize sunglasses. "Oh, hi," she said. "I guess we're busted for bugging out on the group."

Ingrid flipped her thick braid back over her shoulder. "Uh, we didn't really feel like going to a concert, so we skipped off on a side trip. Hope you don't mind."

"No problem," Sam said. "You've been shopping the whole time since the mine tour?"

Daniella groaned inwardly. Too direct.

Whitney cocked her head. "Yes. Why do you ask?"

"Oh, uh, I just like to know these things so I can better plan tours for my guests. Might have to scrap the concert thing."

Quick thinking, Sam.

"Would you like a ride back to the opera house?" he asked.

"No, we're not finished checking out the shops and I want ice cream," Whitney said. "We'll take a taxi back to the lodge."

Daniella tried for a giggle as she looked at Ingrid.

"Your brother wasn't at the opera house. Concerts aren't his thing either?"

A flicker of concern shone for a moment on Ingrid's brow. "No. He doesn't like live music much and he rarely does anything if it doesn't please him. He must have wandered off somewhere." She brightened. "He did say he had some business calls to make. He's probably in a café somewhere where he can get on the internet."

What's his business? She wanted to ask, but that would definitely not be a "nanny" type of question.

They said goodbye.

Sam drove to the lodge, their comfortable chatter ebbing into silence. Oliver fell asleep, dozing with Zara in the back seat, her paw protectively placed on his shin. Daniella could not help but take a picture of the two.

The heat climbed past one hundred and ten, according to her phone app. There was movement in the rocks on the side of the road, perhaps a lizard or rodent. Incredible that mountain lions, black bears and bobcats managed to survive here in the hostile climate, powerful predators suited to their environment. Generally, they relied on laying low during the hottest part of the day.

Human predators were good at surviving and thriving too, she thought, sometimes hiding in plain sight.

On the last bit of steep slope, the tree-lined drive disrupted the sunlight with dark purple shadows. There was a predator on the lodge property. She was sure.

Paul? Ingrid? Whitney? Edward? John? Plenty of suspects and very few answers.

Sam watched as the guests climbed out of the van. All five were present. The women must have returned to the opera house at the appointed hour after their ice cream. Paul too. John barely waited for them all to climb out before he sped off. Daniella was watching also, though anyone else would think she was absorbed in coloring with Oliver on a pad of paper. Zara sat at their feet.

When they assembled for dinner, Daniella and Oliver stayed at the kitchen table, within earshot of the chattering guests. Sam didn't pick up on any helpful information about who could have snuck back to the lodge, and he got more frustrated as the evening wore on. After the meal, the guests departed to their rooms or the courtyard. He gave Mae a hand with the dishes.

He hefted a full bag of trash and headed for the dumpster at the far side of the old lodge. On his way back, he came upon Ingrid and Paul standing in the moonlit courtyard. Her arms were crossed over her chest while he slouched with hands in his pockets.

"I'm not sure anymore," Ingrid said.

"You're never sure of anything," Paul snapped. "But I am, so grow a backbone, why don't you?"

They both turned abruptly at Sam's approach. Ingrid swept a hand to the sky. "Just looking for stars," she said quickly.

"Moonlight's going to interfere with that, I'm afraid," Sam said. "And it's too early to get a good view."

Paul laughed. "That's what I was telling her. Timing is everything, right?"

"Right," Sam said. Returning to the lodge, he shared what he'd heard with Daniella.

"They don't get along well," he said.

"Yet they decided to vacation together," Daniella

said. "Doesn't that strike you as odd? I would never even attempt to vacation with my brother."

"It does." An ominous feeling followed Sam through his evening chores, though Daniella was staying with Oliver while Sam was occupied.

As he made his way to Oliver's room, the lodge was quiet and still.

"Can I have your cell phone?" Daniella asked him.

He handed it over and she installed an app. "You can check the baby monitor from your phone." She held up a finger. "Oh wait. I meant the walkie-talkie. I've got one on mine too for the monitor and the exterior cameras."

"What's the coverage like?"

"There's one in the tree, which captures the side, one on the rear exit door, and one aimed at the front courtyard. Unfortunately, the old lodge is out of view as is the parking lot and the shed. Best we can do for now with three cameras."

"As long as it shows Oliver's window, I'll sleep easier."

Oliver's mouth puckered and he looked like he might cry. "Don't wanna sleep in here," he started then stuck his fingers in his mouth. "The bad man…"

Sam's heart quivered at the fear in Oliver's voice. "That person won't come back. You'll be safe."

"About that," Daniella said, looking from Oliver to Sam. "I was thinking that Zara and I should bunk with Oliver. I can move the futon in here."

Sam frowned.

Oliver nodded, beaming a bright smile at her that was interrupted by a yawn.

It was an odd notion, someone else watching over

his son. Why hesitate? What could be safer for his boy than having a cop and her K-9 sleeping inches away?

"All right," he said. "Let me take care of bath and story time and then I'll move that futon for you. Are you, uh, sure that's what you want to do?"

"Better idea than you sleeping in here, since you have to be up and at 'em at all hours if a guest needs help. I'll keep the baby..." She shot a look at Oliver. "I mean, the walkie-talkie focused on him so you can check any time. Workable?"

Sam blew out a breath. As much as he didn't like giving up control, he had to let her do her job. It was the reason Tyson had sent her, and it was safest for Oliver. He juggled the boy. "Is that okay, if Nanny Ella sleeps in your room with you?"

Daniella smiled at Oliver. "Zara or I will be with you, all the time, okay?"

He brightened. "KK," he said. "Bubbles, Daddy?"

"Yes, we can have bubbles in the tub," Sam said with a smile.

"Um," Daniella said, "you can handle the bath supervision solo. That's not in my wheelhouse, and Zara will want to jump in the tub and make a massive mess."

The knot in Sam's gut relaxed at the giggle from his son as he watched Zara's tail wagging. *Relax*, he told himself. It was okay for Oliver to spend time with another woman. Besides, the boy's clinginess was probably due to fear anyway, rather than fondness.

When Oliver was belly-button deep in bubbles, washing with his dinosaur sponge, Sam listened to him sing the ABCs. "Great job," he said. "You got all the letters, even the *v*. Mommy would be so proud of you."

Oliver stopped humming. "Mommy's gone."

Sam swallowed. "Yes." The water dripping from Oliver's sponge sounded strangely amplified in the quiet.

"Is she coming back?"

He'd heard the question before and it killed him every single time. He pushed out the word. "No, son. Mommy isn't coming back."

Oliver splashed down his sponge, splattering water across the tile floor. "Can Nanny Ella be my mommy?"

He barely restrained his gasp. *No*, he wanted to snap. *No one will take the place of your mother.*

But Hannah was just a name to Oliver, one that was becoming more unfamiliar every day. Pain whipped through Sam like a desert sandstorm.

He distracted Oliver with some dinosaur sponge antics, but a weight had settled in his stomach. Having another woman around was confusing Oliver into thinking she was a mother figure, disrupting the family nest Sam had so painstakingly constructed. Their family felt so very fragile in that instant, like the shifting of one tiny thimbleful of sand might send everything into collapse. He realized he hadn't answered Oliver, who was watching him, waiting.

"Daniella is your nanny. That means she's here to take care of you, but she's not your mommy. Do you understand?"

Oliver nodded, but he was more interested in capturing bubbles in his scooped palms than continuing the conversation. He did not understand in the slightest.

Sam forced himself to relax his jaw, breathe out hard, but urgency punched at him. He had to do whatever he could to help capture the marauding guest quickly. Then Daniella would leave and their lives would get back to normal. In the meantime, he'd keep reminding himself that though he enjoyed being close to her, it was imperative to keep things professional.

He plastered on a smile, coaxed his son from the water, dried him off, and wrapped him in a robe before walking him to his room. "I'll be right in to help you get your pj's on." Daniella gave him a thumbs-up to indicate she would keep eyes on him.

Sam took the futon from the room he'd assigned Daniella and carried it to Oliver's. There, he found her standing next to his son as he struggled to pull on his pajama top. The boy was squirming, attempting to jam his head into the correct hole. Sam moved to help him, but Daniella held up a finger.

"He's almost got it," she said.

"I…" Sam watched openmouthed as Oliver wriggled, grunted and pulled on the top. His hair stood up and a wide grin split his face as he pumped his arms in victory.

"High five," he demanded, shoving a small palm at Daniella, who slapped it gently.

"High five, Zara," Daniella commanded, and Zara lifted her paw to receive Oliver's pat, which sent the boy into a fit of giggles.

Sam was speechless.

Daniella cut a glance at him. "You look mad. Did I overstep or something?" she whispered.

"No," he whispered back stiffly. "It's fine."

Her brow quirked. "You don't look like it's fine."

"No problem. Really." He turned away and fussed with the bedding so she wouldn't see his discomfiture. So Oliver had accomplished dressing himself. So what? Nothing that should prove upsetting. "Story time, son."

Oliver climbed into bed and selected one of his arsenal of dinosaur books. Danielle moved toward the door. Sam was glad. Her proximity confused and troubled him. "It was a sunny day in dino land…" he started.

"Nanny Ella," Oliver cried out as Daniella strolled to the threshold. "You're 'posed to stay." His voice was pitched high with the beginnings of hysteria.

"Uh…" Daniella said, looking from Sam to Oliver and back again. "I figured maybe this was a daddy-son thing. I was going to wait outside with Zara. She pants real loud, so that might mess up story time."

Stop being a dolt, Sam said to himself. He gestured to the rocking chair. "No need to leave. This story is a real winner," he managed to blurt out. "You won't want to miss it."

Silently, she sat with Zara, mute until he came to the end, not even commenting when Oliver pointed out that he'd skipped a line. They finished with the prayer he'd taught his son. The one his father had taught him and he and Hannah had said at Oliver's crib side until she was too sick to endure it. *Lord*, he added, *please help me raise this boy the way You want.*

Had he been doing that? Or was he too focused on trying to imbue his son with perceptions of Hannah? Coddling him too much? His head spun. He wound up the wooden music box he'd cobbled together that played a happy tune, another ritual his son insisted upon.

He gave Oliver a kiss on the forehead and headed toward the door.

Daniella stood, checking her cell phone. "Let's hope my cameras aren't spotted," she whispered.

Cameras. His brain fastened on the word. With those in place, they'd stand a chance of capturing their would-be stalker and he and his boy could pick up their lives where they'd left off.

She touched his arm. A tingle erupted along his skin at the feel of her warm fingertips. She stepped into the hall and he followed her.

"I apologize if I did something wrong," she said. Her eyes were black satin, her expressive mouth pulled into a half frown that tugged at his heart. "I'm not known for being sensitive. I gotta work on it."

"You didn't do anything wrong. I… I might be guilty of doing too much for him. I try to think…" He trailed off.

"What Hannah would do?"

"Yes."

Danielle nodded. "How old was he when she died?"

"Eight months."

The hall light played against the soft curve of her cheek and he felt the unexpected desire to reach out and stroke her skin.

"Eight months," she said quietly. "They're not even walking yet. That's rough—her dying when he was so young. So you're trying to create memories for him through yours."

Sam felt like he'd been slapped. But there was nothing cruel in her words, in the frank curiosity in her eyes. Spoken aloud, it sounded wrong, as if he were forcing something on his son. "I…" His comment trailed off. "I guess so."

"That's a lot of pressure on you both. If he doesn't make memories of his mom, then you feel like you betrayed your wife."

What had her comment sent racing through his nerves? Anger? Irritation? Anxiety? It was suddenly too much. "I'd better go prepare the coffee for tomorrow. Big day with the Gila Wilderness hike."

He could not get away fast enough. Her words burned fiery circles inside him. He'd never considered that his dogged determination to forge memories of Hannah in Oliver's heart might be a form of pressure. *No*, he said in silent savagery. It was what had to happen. Oliver had to remember the woman who gave him life, the mother who'd loved him with a desperation that fueled her grueling fight against cancer.

He remembered the sheer grin of delight when Oliver had high-fived Daniella and her dog, and his own electric thrill at being close to the dark-eyed cop.

Whatever is happening here, you need to stop it right now.

Hastening his steps, he jogged down the stairwell.

He hoped the cameras would help them capture the bad guys and he'd bring Oliver's life back on track.

I'll make sure Oliver is safe, Hannah.

Hope was all he had.

Daniella rocked in the squeaky chair beside Oliver's bed. She'd installed the locked gun box on the top shelf of the closet while Oliver was asleep. Even if he somehow found it, he would never be able to open it to access the weapon. Agitation fueled her rocking, and she determined she needed to add a similar chair to her sparsely furnished Denver apartment. Her conversation with Sam replayed on an endless loop. She'd been trying to understand, not judge, but her words had come out wrong, as they usually did when the topic was emotions.

"It's his son and his life, so do your job and butt out," she murmured to herself, earning a look from Zara, who had inched as close to Oliver's bed as she could. She'd let Zara have her beloved Nettie, which was tucked between her front paws. Midnight the cat had snuck in earlier and was sitting on the shelf below the window, watching Zara with outright hostility. Zara would answer with a tail wag anytime she noticed Midnight staring. But so far the cat had not warmed to the dog.

Might as well use the time to research the guests. When she ran into a dead end, she texted Jodie Chen, RMK9 Unit assistant and her best friend.

I need help. Getting nowhere fast with this investigation.

Jodie texted back.

Got something for you, but first how's the nanny gig going?

She was surprised at the pang of pain as she considered how she'd upset Sam. He was a good father, a good man, and his kid was darling. Guilt left a bitter taste in her mouth.

I think I've offended the dad. Shot my mouth off.

I'm sure you didn't. You're just a bit direct sometimes.

Daniella smiled. She and Jodie were 180-degree opposites. Jodie's enthusiastic and tender nature was a complete contrast to Daniella's sardonic temperament. She remembered the day she'd seen Jodie visiting Shiloh, the year-old black Lab in training at the RMK9

Unit campus to possibly become a K-9, telling the dog in sign language that she loved him, like her deaf parents had done with her. She'd had to remind Jodie not to get too attached to Shiloh since, if he passed training, he'd be assigned to work with a handler.

I'll try to keep my filter in place. What have you got on the guests?

Another message materialized from Jodie.

Ingrid checks out as having attended same university as Hannah Kavanaugh. Paul is her younger half brother, no records or warrants, nothing on the radar from either of them. They both lived in Germany during their college years. Edward Reese has no record or priors. He's worked for an insurance company for the past four years. The only loose end is that I can't find a current teaching credential for Ingrid.

What about John Payat?

He's got a prior for petty theft. He worked for a construction company and stole some materials. Did eighteen months before he was released. Nothing since.

Interesting.

And the newlyweds?

Still working on that. Things have been uber-tense around here with SAC Michael Bridges asking questions about everything from how we handle cases to the dog training schedule. He makes me jumpy. Will message when I get something.

Daniella tapped out a reply.

All right. Thanks for the info. Tennis match when I get back?

Never again, you're too competitive. Brings out your ferocious streak. Movies, and you're buying the popcorn since I'm doing all this work for you. Gonna want a giant tub with extra butter. And chocolate-covered raisins. And a soda. And refills if necessary.

Daniella stifled a laugh.

Done. Talk to you later.

Oliver shifted in his sleep, and Zara raised her nose, again offering a hopeful wag toward the cat. It would take them both some time to adjust to the normal sleeping sounds of a preschooler. She hoped he didn't wake up because she had no idea how to soothe a kid in the night.

Opening the tiny tattered Bible that was never far out of reach, she found a scripture Uncle Cal had recited to her again and again. Zara cocked her head expectantly as Daniella read.

"'In the world ye shall have tribulation: but be of good cheer; I have overcome the world.'" She eyed the dog. "Hear that? We're gonna make it through this tribulation, girl. Promise."

Zara let out a soft huff of air that ruffled her lips.

With a start, she realized Oliver had been listening too, and now he was sitting up in bed, looking alarmingly alert.

"Sorry, I woke you," she whispered. "Go back to sleep now."

"Can't," Oliver said. "My eyes are awake."

No arguing with that logic. "Well, if you lie down, you'll fall right back asleep."

Oliver sighed. "I'm 'fraid of the bad man."

Daniella thought a moment. "Let's try something," she said. "My friend's Mommy and Daddy can't hear, so they talk using their hands. She taught me this word." She made two fists and slid them away from each other. "It means safe. Can you do it?"

He did, a mystified look on his face.

Daniella nodded encouragement. "If you feel scared in the night, make that sign to yourself and you'll remember that you're safe. You can show Zara too."

Delighted, Oliver demonstrated. Zara licked him on the wrist.

"Good. Here's the other sign." She held Oliver's tiny palm in hers and laid her own hand in it, two fingers crooked into a *v* on top of it. "This means 'lie down.' See? Like a person lying in their bed. Show me 'safe' and 'lie down.'" He did and she gave him a thumbs-up. "All right. I'm going to sit here in the rocking chair and, if you wake up, show me the sign for safety."

He nodded and she gave him the "lie down" sign. He did and, after fifteen minutes or so, he fell asleep.

Wait until I tell Jodie about this.

Before Daniella settled on the futon, she set an alarm to wake her every three hours so she could check the cameras. Unnecessary, as she slept fitfully. Whenever she jolted to wakefulness, she found herself thinking about Sam. She'd upset him, no matter what he said. By encouraging Oliver to dress himself? Who didn't want their kid to be self-sufficient?

Her mind traveled back into the past. She thought about her own baby, the one she'd given birth to at the tender age of sixteen before Uncle Cal had changed her life and taught her about God.

If Daniella had tried to raise her daughter, would she have coddled her as Sam seemed to do? Then again, maybe his coddling was just normal loving. She wouldn't know, her parents being what they were. And who was she to pass judgment on a parent trying their best every day to do something she couldn't?

It bothered her that she'd upset Sam, and that worried her. Tough, independent, no-nonsense Daniella shouldn't care about anything but getting the job done. That's why she was there, no other reason. She forced her eyes closed but sleep refused to come. At a little after 3:00 a.m., she checked the cameras again.

Movement.

She jerked up like a jack-in-the-box, pulse racing. Zara went stiff-eared. Maybe it was an animal, a bobcat or coyote. She stared some more at the tiny screen. In the shadows near the front door, a shape materialized, moving slowly toward the old lodge.

Definitely a human shape.

Silently she retrieved her weapon.

Bring it on, tribulation. I'm coming for you.

SIX

The squeak of a floorboard pulled Sam from a restless sleep long before dawn. Bleary-eyed, he fumbled for the video monitor. Oliver was snoozing peacefully, his shaggy blond hair visible from under the blanket in the glow of the stegosaurus night-light. Zara was now sitting on Oliver's bed, her eyes open. Midnight would be furious.

Sam exhaled. With a police Malinois sharing a mattress with Oliver, there could be no safer situation for his son. On the screen Zara looked around, ears swiveling. Had something set the dog on edge?

Sam strained to listen. A second squeak brought him to his feet. Someone was up and about, moving toward the lower level. Probably the noise had a purely innocent cause. Daniella out patrolling or a guest in search of a midnight snack since he always provided a charcuterie selection in the refrigerator.

Considering the circumstances, he wasn't about to let the noises go by uninvestigated. Throwing on jeans and a sweatshirt, he shoved his feet into his battered leather boots and padded across the floor, easing the knob open. He'd left the door to his room unlocked in case Daniella or Oliver needed anything in the night.

The air-conditioned stairwell was cool, the chill contained by the thick adobe walls that also served to keep the ferocious Santa Fe heat at bay. He worked his way along, checking the guest room doors, which were all closed. The library was quiet. The windows were locked, as they should be, except for the one that would not latch properly. He peered out the window down into the darkened courtyard.

Below he could make out the dim porch light of the old lodge. In the bushes to the right of the front porch, a tiny blue light flickered for a moment before it was extinguished. Daniella probably, checking. He should leave her to her night patrolling. She was a cop after all.

But then he saw another light, larger, moving around the other side of the property. A flashlight? There was insufficient camera coverage there to feed images of the intruder to Daniella. She would be taken completely by surprise. His breath froze in his lungs. He reached to text her and recalled that he'd left his phone by his bed. *Lughead.* By the time he fetched it, Daniella might be hurt or worse.

He made his decision, ran downstairs through the kitchen, grabbing the first thing he saw to use as a weapon. His cast-iron frying pan. Oliver would be safe with Zara guarding him. Sam had to warn Daniella.

"What are you doing?"

Sam whirled to see Edward Reese in the kitchen, dressed in shorts and a T-shirt.

"I could ask you the same thing," Sam said.

He shrugged. "Looking for that charcuterie platter in the fridge." He eyed the frying pan. "Somehow I don't think you're fixing to fry up some eggs. What's wrong?"

"Nothing," Sam said, trying to keep his voice steady. "I'm going to check on something outside."

Edward raised a brow. "And you grabbed a cast-iron pan to do that?" He paused. "Need some backup?"

"No," Sam said, forcing a smile. "Enjoy the snack. There's a pitcher of tea in the fridge too."

Without waiting any longer, Sam raced into the night.

He charged as quietly as he could up the path, stopping behind a thick pine to reconnoiter. Again, he saw both the flicker of blue and the bobbing flashlight beam. Was the small light Daniella's? Had to be. She'd never be so careless as to advertise her presence with a flashlight. Should he go warn her? No. Go after the flashlight, he decided, rather than risk surprising an armed undercover cop.

Sweat dampened his neck. He skirted the lodge quickly, grateful that he knew every rock and dip along the way. A few yards from the porch, he pulled up in the deep shadows of a pine. What he wouldn't give for a pair of army-issue night-vision binoculars. Whoever it was must be wearing a dark hat and clothes because Sam could not see the slightest glimpse of them. He waited, heart whamming against his ribs. Wood groaned with an almost human quality, the sound stopping immediately. It was all the information Sam needed. He knew that groan had issued from the warped screen-room door being eased open. How many times had he applied WD-40 to those hinges with no success?

The intruder must have jimmied the flimsy lock on the handle.

Sam raised the frying pan and shuffled slowly along

the pine-needle-covered path. Inside the screen room, he could make out the flashlight beam dancing across the boxes stored there. He inched closer. The screened area opened up into the main house via an interior wooden door, but so far the intruder was busily scanning the boxes. Did he or she have a weapon? Sam crept another step closer and gently gripped the screen door latch with one hand, the fry pan gripped in the other.

Gotcha, he said to himself. As he leaned forward, a twig snapped under his foot.

The searcher stopped and straightened, the flashlight beam suddenly turning in Sam's direction. Before Sam could decide what to do next, the door was flung open, propelling him backward onto the dirt. Rolling to his stomach, he was trying to get up when a booted foot kicked him in the shoulder. The blow glanced off without only a dull stab of pain, but it cost Sam a few precious seconds to right himself. He lunged for the ankles of the intruder, but his fingers grazed a pant leg. It was enough to cause the intruder to stumble.

Praying it bought him the seconds he needed, Sam surged into action.

Service revolver drawn, Daniella burst through the interior wood door into the screen room. Empty. A grunt from outside propelled her onward. She ran into the side yard. In the darkness, she glimpsed someone rising from the ground.

"Stop! Police!" she yelled.

The figure froze, hands up. "Daniella…"

She reflexively stepped back. "Sam?"

"Yeah." He pointed. "Bad guy ran into the woods.

East. Toward the gate into the Gila. We've gotta hurry. Once he gets in there, we'll lose him for sure."

"You hurt?"

"No." He stooped and grabbed something from the ground. "Come on."

"I've got this," Daniella insisted. "Go back to the lodge."

"Not gonna happen." His face was like a slab of hardened granite in the dim light as he quickly checked his phone. "Zara is with Oliver. I know every square inch of this property. You're wasting time. Let's move."

Did he think he could give her orders? He was a civilian after all and this work was firmly in her sphere not his. She opened her mouth to argue, but he was already hustling up the path, half jogging under the canopy of trees, remarkably quiet for a man his size.

She had no choice but to bite back her scathing retort, holster her weapon and run after him. He'd get a piece of her mind later, she decided.

With only a sliver of moon to light the way, the path posed a challenge. She kept near Sam as he dodged various obstacles including a fallen log that they had to climb over.

He pulled to a stop at the apex of the trail. "Up here. High enough to get a good look." He dropped the pan he'd been carrying and climbed atop a flat granite rock the size of her cop car, pausing to offer her a palm.

Practicality before pride, she told herself as he hauled her up.

They knelt on the rock shelf, scanning the wilderness below. She tried to regulate her breathing, not wanting him to hear her panting from the thin air. They flopped onto their stomachs, staring down into what must be the Gila National Forest. Silvery trails stretched beneath them, eventually swallowed up by velvet darkness. Wind swirled the branches and crackles from the rocky ground indicated small animals were on the prowl. Far away, a coyote howled, the keening mournful.

"Gone," Sam snarled. "There are a zillion hiding places and obscure routes that lead back to the lodge."

"I don't suppose we can conduct a fire drill back at the Cliffside so we could count heads?"

He grimaced. "That would damage our reputation with the guests. I can't really afford to do that."

The furrow on his brow showed clearly in the moonlight. They'd experienced yet another lead that had slipped through their fingers. He was angry, but not defeated. From what she knew of Sam, he'd fight and scrap to make the best of what God had given him, just like she had.

She climbed to her feet to dispel the strange fuzzy feeling in her belly. "Well, it looks like we lost our man, or woman, again. Let's get back to the lodge and maybe we'll catch a break and spot someone returning."

Climbing down, she landed wrong and stumbled. He grabbed her arm to steady her, and she was drawn against his broad chest. The same strange electricity shot through her. It was a dizzying sense that she belonged near Sam. She quickly detached herself. *Straighten up, Vargas. You going soft or something?* "It's clear they want something that you have, Sam. Something here on your property. What is it?"

He shook his head. "I have no idea."

She cocked her head, still searching herself for her rock-solid identity. She wasn't a softie, not by a long shot and there was no room for the nebulous feelings

Sam seemed to awaken in her. She had to push him if they were going to wrap up this case. "Are you sure?"

He stared at her. "What do you mean *am I sure*?"

She pressed on. "Are you keeping something from me? Maybe you have valuables here you don't want to disclose?"

His eyes rounded. "Are you kidding? This is my life we're talking about, and my son's. Do you think for one minute I'm lying to you when Oliver's in danger?"

"I'm not saying you're lying…"

"That's exactly what you're saying," he snapped. "You think I would put my son at risk?" His voice raised an octave, steeped in anger. "If that's the case, then you don't know me at all, Officer Vargas."

He snatched the pan from the ground and stalked down the path.

Way to go, Daniella. The worst of it was that she did know deep down that Sam was not hiding anything from her. Why had she needed him to say it? She hurried to catch him. "Wait," she said, grasping his shoulder.

He shook her off. She skirted around him, blocking his way, palms up.

"I'm sorry." Her apology seemed to surprise him as much as it did her. "It was a dumb question, and I shouldn't have asked it. I know you would never endanger Oliver even if the lost treasure of the Aztecs was at stake." She paused. "Forgive me?" Suddenly, it was of ultimate importance that he did.

The crease between his brows deepened.

Please forgive me, her brain cried out; and she could not understand the quivering mass that throbbed where her heart should be. What was wrong with her? Sam had done more than gotten under her skin. He seemed to have burrowed right into her heart.

He looked at his feet, frying pan dangling from his lowered hand. After a long, slow breath, he raised his head. "I do. And I should probably ask your forgiveness too. I barged into your operation. Maybe messed things up. Could be if I'd stayed in the lodge you would have bagged the culprit yourself."

She let out a measured sigh. "Why did you barge in, by the way? You think I can't handle it?"

"No, not that." He shrugged. "I saw from the library window what was going on. I was afraid he'd take you by surprise and you'd get hurt."

Her breath grew shallow. "You were worried about me?"

He paused. "Yes."

This man was worried she'd get hurt. Outside of colleagues and Uncle Cal, when was the last time a man had cared about her that much?

The moment stretched long between them. "Oh. Well. Thank you," she managed to say over a sudden cascade of butterflies tickling her stomach. How odd. Sure, her police compatriots were always watching her back and her uncle cared deeply for her physical welfare, but aside from casual dating experiences she'd never had a man appear to be honestly concerned about her well-being. "That's, um, nice," she said awkwardly. "Let's walk back now," she added quickly.

He nodded and, side by side, they headed back to the lodge. He rested the heavy pan on his shoulder.

"Uh…you came to protect me armed with a frying pan?" she said.

His chuckle blended with the pine needles fluttering in the breeze. "All I could find."

She laughed. "Never underestimate the power of good cookware."

"Truth." When his chuckle died away, he grew serious. "Edward Reese was in the kitchen," he said, his stride slowing for a minute. "Said he was looking for a snack. He knew I was up to something, even though I tried to put him off. Since he clearly wasn't the one breaking into the old lodge, I figured he was in the clear, but it occurs to me…"

"That he might have warned whoever was searching the screen room," she finished.

"Exactly what I was thinking," Sam said.

So, Edward Reese was still firmly on the suspect list. Two steps forward, she thought, and a giant step back. "What's on deck for tomorrow?"

"Taking the visitors into the Gila for some early morning hiking." He shot her a look. "Oliver is coming too. No way am I leaving him behind."

"I figured. Zara and I will be there also, of course, which leaves the lodge unprotected."

"Mae will be here changing the bedding and starting dinner. Will that present any danger to her?"

Daniella mentally cautioned herself to be sensitive. "I can take some precautions and leave her with my cell number. Call in a favor to local PD to come by and check." Here it goes. "Sam, I know you've worked with Mae for a long time. I'm not impugning her character, or anything, just doing my job. Do you trust her?" She was surprised that he grinned at her.

"That was very sensitively put, Officer Vargas."

She felt the strange fluttering confusion in her stomach again. "Well, um, I'm trying."

He reached out and squeezed an arm around her shoulders. Just a quick pressure and release, but it was the best feeling she'd experienced in as long as she could remember. *Daniella*...she cautioned herself again, but he was replying.

"The week I lost Hannah, Oliver must have been teething or something, because he would cry on and off all night long. I was numb, in shock maybe. I..." He gulped. "My in-laws were trying to get to us to help, but it was during a terrible rainy season and the road to the lodge was impassable, so the family was delayed several days in arriving. I was up all night, walking the floors, and I felt like I was mentally disintegrating. I texted Mae to ask for advice on how to calm him down, but cell service must have been touch and go because she didn't respond. Oliver just cried and cried, and it seemed like there was nothing I could do to soothe him."

Daniella glanced at him and could tell he was deep into the memory.

"I remember putting him down in his crib and laying facedown on the floor," he continued, "sobbing louder than he was. Then I noticed that I'd gotten a text back from Mae. She'd said she was on her way, that her son would drive her to the lodge in his off-road vehicle. She was staying, whether I agreed or not. She brought groceries, diapers, blankets, and she moved herself into my son's room, took the night shift until I could function. If that isn't enough to convince you of her character, I don't know what is."

Daniella heard the catch in his voice. "It's enough," she said, mentally scratching Mae off the suspect list.

Part of her still wrestled with what had just occurred. Sam had put himself at risk with only a fry pan as a weapon because he'd been worried for her safety. And she'd responded by basically accusing him of concealing something from her. If there was a booklet on how to drive people away, she could probably be a coauthor. And, anyway, he was just being kind and cautious, because that's the kind of man he was.

As they approached the lodge, she made sure her revolver was covered by the hem of her T-shirt. *You're a nanny, remember? Do the job. That's why you're here.*

But if she'd been spotted by the screen-room burglar, then her cover was already blown.

Fine, she decided. If the stalker knew she was a cop, then he or she had gotten the message loud and clear. No one was going to hurt Sam or Oliver. Not on her watch.

SEVEN

Saturday morning Sam helped Mae scramble eggs and fry the locally made sausage patties for breakfast. He'd cheated and ordered a delivery of muffins from a bakery in town since the ongoing investigation was keeping him from his normal cooking duties.

He checked the clock again. Only Edward and Matthew were seated at the table so far. Could the reason for the women's absence be they'd been responsible for the screen-room burglary? Or was it simply that it was barely 6:00 a.m.? Santa Fe temperatures required that strenuous hiking be done as early in the day as possible, which was tough on folks who weren't morning people. He fussed with the buffet table, wondering if their plans were about to go up in smoke. A memory poked at him, leftover from when he'd peeked into Oliver's room the previous night to find him sound asleep, Daniella in the rocking chair, and Zara watching over them both. They'd looked so tranquil, as if they belonged together. He tried to shake off the thought.

Daniella and Zara escorted Oliver to the kitchen table. Oliver was holding on to Daniella's three middle fingers. When he climbed into his seat, she filled his plate with food and set it in front of him before she fed Zara and started in on her own meal.

Things were so natural between them, this woman and his son. Why did it give him a pang that they looked comfortable together? And why did he find his spirits lifting when he returned Daniella's smile with one of his own? He'd seen a humble, sensitive side to her when she'd asked him to forgive her the previous night, and it had changed his perception of her.

"Coffee," Mae said, poking him in the shoulder.

"What?"

"You were going to refill the coffeepot, hon. Best not to run out until they're fully fueled."

He realized he'd been so lost in his thoughts about Daniella he'd completely forgotten his errand. "Right."

Coffee carafes filled, he greeted Whitney and Ingrid as they strolled in.

Whitney yawned and raked her long blond hair away from her forehead. "I'm not in a hiking mood. I want to stay behind."

He froze. To give herself an opportunity to snoop around?

Matthew shook his head. "Oh no, honey. You're not weaseling out of this. It was your idea to come to this lodge, and you said we'd hike. I even bought new hiking boots." He filled his coffee cup and added a dollop of cream. "We have to have some good pictures for social media. You'll feel more inspired after breakfast." He fetched her a cup of coffee with cream and an added spoonful of sugar. "Whitney is not a fan of mornings unless they start at eleven," he said to Sam.

She scowled, but to Sam's relief, her expression softened and she allowed her husband to kiss her cheek when he handed her the coffee. "All right. Hopefully it will be worth it."

"I want to take some pictures of the patio garden in the morning light before I eat," Ingrid said. "I'll be right back." Her dark hair was neatly braided and her clothes tidy, but there was an air of exhaustion about her, smudged shadows that spoke of a restless night. How restless? he wondered. He thought back to her argument with her brother, when Paul had told her to "grow a backbone."

Daniella caught Ingrid's comment too and they both watched as the woman meandered into the courtyard where Paul was waiting. He appeared chipper and relaxed, seated with one booted foot propped up on the edge of the fire pit.

Sam could not make out their conversation, even with the bay windows thrown wide to catch the morning cool, but Ingrid's arms went around her waist in a self hug as she regarded her brother.

"Tension there," Daniella whispered, startling him.

He turned and found her so close he could have embraced her. For one unsettling moment, he realized he wanted to do exactly that. Embrace her? What? Confused, he stepped back, bumping an indoor plant and sending it teetering. Daniella caught it and set it back on its pottery feet.

"I'll be right back," she said, quietly telling Zara to stay with Oliver. "I think I left one of Zara's balls outside," she said for the benefit of the guests.

"And I have to replace the wood in the fire pit." He hurried out the door before she could dissuade him.

He puttered around on his march to the woodpile. Daniella kept her distance from Ingrid and Paul, hunting under bushes but not close enough to disrupt the conversation. Their backs were to Sam and Daniella. Sam figured he'd leave the eavesdropping to Daniella and see what he could make of the body language. One phrase leaped to his ear regardless.

"Not right," Ingrid said. "I don't want you to do that."

Do what? Sam wrestled a stack of logs and Ingrid finally caught sight of him. She poked her brother, who shot a lazy look at Sam before returning his attention to his sister.

"Big sister—" he got up "—you are not my boss," he said to her before bobbing his chin at Sam.

Daniella straightened, holding a squashed plastic ball with multiple teeth punctures. "Good morning," she said.

"Morning," Paul returned. "Your dog has some impressive jaw power," he said as he looked at the ball.

"Yes, she does. That's why Malinois are nicknamed 'maligators.'"

His look grew thoughtful, amused. "No offense, but isn't it weird for a nanny to have such an aggressive dog?"

Sam tightened his grip on the wood and moved to the fire pit. Did Paul know that Daniella was a cop?

Daniella laughed, appearing not the least bit stressed. "Zara's not aggressive, unless she has a reason to be. And she adores kids."

Mouth quirked, Paul nodded. "Whatever floats your boat, I guess. See you inside, sis." Paul returned to the house.

Ingrid didn't move as Sam refilled the wood in the fire pit. Did she remain to enjoy the morning cool and the hint of gold that splayed across the horizon? Or was she troubled at her conversation with her sibling?

"Is everything okay?" Sam asked her.

She shrugged. "Yes. My fault that I'm out of sorts. It was harder than I thought to come here and see the life that Hannah made." Her eyes glistened. "We didn't have enough time together, and I wasn't as good a friend as I should have been. I miss her."

The comment shocked Sam in the gut. "I miss her too."

"She was so excited when she wrote me about being pregnant. I never would have imagined... I mean she was so young and you'd only just gotten married. I thought we had all the time in the world to catch up again."

He poked at the wood, settling it into a pile. He'd thought the same; a lifetime at least with his effervescent Hannah. He'd come to a place of acceptance that God had not saved his wife, but he certainly didn't understand it. The definition of faith, he thought. To trust, even when you don't understand. But trusting didn't mean it didn't hurt, sometimes more than he could stand.

"It might have been a mistake coming here," Ingrid said. "Especially with Paul. He was sick too, when he was a baby, almost died. Everyone catered to him and he thinks that's the way things should be all the time. I forgot how annoying it is to travel with him." She sighed and a mischievous smile bloomed on her face. "Don't tell Paul, but I really am the boss whether he likes it or not."

Sam allowed a chuckle. Daniella tossed the ball from palm to palm.

Ingrid lifted her chin. "Brother or not, I'm looking forward to seeing the cliff dwellings. I want to take pictures for the students I'll have when we start school in the fall." Enthusiasm shone on her face. "That is, if I can get my credential renewed. I've moved, so I had some classes to make up."

That explained why Daniella's contacts, including fellow K-9 officer Chris Fuller, hadn't found a current teaching credential on file for Ingrid. She'd had a quick conversation with Chris. He was busy, dealing with the aftermath of saving a woman's life, searching for the missing baby, and the discovery of another potential victim of a serial killer who disappeared in a wildnerness area in Utah.

"Just take things slow," Chris had advised about Daniella's case. "Don't try to make the facts fit your theories just because you want to get out of there."

Busted, she thought, her attention turning back to Sam.

"Lots of great photo ops," Sam said. "The Gila is one of the few places you can actually hike up to the ancient dwellings. Weather permitting, we've got a guided tour arranged for tomorrow up to the ruins after you've rested up from the hike."

"Weather?"

"There's a storm in the forecast. They can be vicious in this area."

"This is the only vacation I'm likely to get for a while, so I'm ready for anything. I'm going to slather on sunscreen and grab some breakfast before we hit the road." Her step was light as she returned to the lodge.

"What do you make of that?" Sam said.

Daniella continued to toss and catch the ball in her

palm. "Could be legit. My brother and I wouldn't last long as traveling partners."

"Do you have much contact with him?"

She shrugged. "Uncle Cal helped us reconnect, but I'm not…er, great at relationships. Working on it." She caught the ball and gazed at the lodge.

"Do you think Ingrid is telling the truth about why she's here?" Sam asked.

"Until I have reason to prove her story, no. They're all potentially involved."

He sighed. "I was thinking the exact opposite. Until there's reason to doubt her, I'd default to believing that she has nothing to do with what's happening here."

She chucked him the ball and he caught it, barely. "That's why you're Captain Sunshine and you need a cynical nanny. Let's go."

Chuckling, he followed her to the lodge. Cynical is what he'd thought of her too, until recently. The way she held Oliver's hand, the way his own pulse double-timed when she was close to him… It all added up to one mixed-up mess. Fortunately, there was plenty of work waiting for him to distract his brain from that line of thinking.

When breakfast was cleared away, he said goodbye to Mae and grabbed the keys to the SUV. Since two vehicles were required, John arrived to drive the lodge van. He stamped into the kitchen to fill his thermos, yawning widely. He did wink at Daniella, but that was the extent of his efforts at sociability.

"Who's riding with me?" he demanded.

The guests snatched up hats and sunglasses, along with their backpacks, and bottled water. Sam had distributed paper sacks with more water, sandwiches, trail mix, fruit and Mae's snickerdoodles.

"Oliver, let's get some sunscreen on you," he called in the kitchen.

"Already done," Daniella said. "And I added bug spray for good measure."

Again he felt the twin pangs of pleasure and concern. She was mommying his boy. "Oh. Great. Thanks." He, Oliver, Daniella and Zara climbed into the SUV. Whitney and Matt had a quick chat and Matt walked her back to the house to retrieve her bug repellent. The others piled into the van John was driving. Daniella gave Zara the chewed-up ball and she tucked it happily under her chin, pushing her hairy torso as close as possible to Oliver's legs while they waited for Whitney and Matt.

"What's the itinerary?" she said.

"We're escorting them to the overlook at the entrance to Gila National park so they can get acclimated. After that, they're on their own to hike wherever they'd like."

"If we hang around a while, we can at least track the direction they head off."

"Right," he said. "That's the plan. John will have the van waiting to pick them up at noon to return them to the lodge or escort them into town for an excursion if they'd rather."

Daniella nodded. "Important thing is that this time no one will have the opportunity to sneak back to the lodge since we'll be there watching for them. I'm going to do some deeper research into Paul and Ingrid. Time's getting short."

Short indeed, he thought. Matt and Whitney would be checking out Wednesday after their week's stay and Ingrid, Paul and Edward would leave on the weekend. If no progress was made, they might depart without Sam and Daniella ever learning the source of the threat. No guarantees whoever it was wouldn't find a way to return. Urgency tightened his gut.

He glanced at Daniella who was looking intently out the window, brows drawn in thought.

And she'd be leaving too.

Maybe that would resolve the puzzling feelings he'd been experiencing. Like the one he was having right then…the sudden flash of sadness at the thought she'd disappear from his life.

Just drive, Sam.
Drive.

Daniella found the sheer scope of the Gila Wilderness park hard to fathom. More than 500,000 acres, twenty-seven miles north to south, thirty-nine east to west. The place was a vast roadless realm with four mountain ranges; no motorized vehicles allowed. Occasionally she got a quick glimpse of one of the hundreds of trails that crisscrossed the wilderness, but most were obscured by juniper woodland and ponderosa pine. The higher elevations bristled with spruce-fir forests. *Pristine* was the word that came to mind…and hot.

"We've got everything here in the Gila," Sam said as they approached the parking lot near the overlook. "Mountain meadows, forest glades, canyons. You'd love the hiking. That feeling of being immersed in God's creation is incomparable." He darted a look at her. "Am I gushing? Sorry."

"No reason to be sorry." As a matter of fact, his description had awakened a longing that she could not brush aside. All her life she'd craved living in such a

place. Exploring the wilderness would be the blessing of a lifetime. She tensed as she realized she'd been
imagining herself exploring it with Sam. A ridiculous
notion. She was here to solve a case and leave. She'd
likely never see Sam or Oliver again.

She shifted on the seat. She'd not allowed herself
to imagine a long-term relationship with any man, let
alone a man with a kid. She'd made her decision about
parenthood long ago. So what in the world was her mind
doing to her now? There was nothing between her and
Sam. He'd not hinted there ever would be. She was relieved when they parked at the overlook, a waist-high
stone wall surrounded by a cement observation deck.
The sun was breaking fully over the massive landscape
and the guests eagerly piled out of the van and scur-
ried to get a look.

Sam took Oliver out and Daniella freed Zara, track-
ing the guests as they emerged from the lodge van.

Ingrid seemed to be chatting with Edward Reese,
leaving Paul to study the view alone. Would she ditch
her brother to hike with Edward? Whitney and Matthew
stood shoulder to shoulder, shading their eyes as they
surveyed the surroundings. Sam distributed trail maps.

Zara barked. Daniella immediately looked for Oliver. He was trying to get a foothold in the rock wall to
boost himself.

"Oliver," Sam said in a firm fatherly voice. "Come
down from there please." The boy still strained to get
a leg up. Danielle moved toward Oliver but a group
of tourists from another lodge disembarked, crowding the space.

"Look," Oliver shouted, pointing to a vulture that
flew so low the flap of its wings was audible.

The guests and the visitors from the other lodges gathered around to see. Daniella was already pushing forward to get to Oliver, but Sam barreled in, linebacker style, shouting an "Excuse me."

Zara had finally run out of patience waiting for the humans. She seized Oliver's pant leg and pulled him down safely to the ground. Daniella breathed a sigh of relief. Oliver was secure.

But Sam wasn't.

There was a flurry of movement, a parting of the crowd. She saw to her horror that Sam had somehow lurched forward over the wall. His fingers sought for a handhold, but it was a futile effort. He tumbled over the wall, plunging out of sight.

EIGHT

Someone screamed, but Daniella hardly registered it.
Even as she shoved through the crowd, her senses were
trying to absorb what she'd just witnessed. Sam had
fallen? How? The "how" could wait until she'd gotten
him back. With one hand, she pulled Oliver away from
the crowd and onto a shaded spot of flat ground with a
cement picnic table.

"Guard," she said to Zara who had already backed
Oliver up against the table, putting her body between
the boy and the spectators. Zara would not allow Oliver to go anywhere else until she was commanded to,
nor would she let someone approach.

"Daddy," Oliver whispered. His eyes were enormous,
beginning to fill with tears.

She took his small hand in hers. "I'm going to help
your daddy. You stay with Zara until I get back, okay?"

On impulse, she kissed his forehead and squeezed
him close for a moment, trying to say with her touch
what she couldn't capture in words.

John Payat appeared at her elbow, mouth open.

"Stay here and watch Oliver, okay?" she commanded.

He grimaced. "With that dog standing there?"

"Don't approach him, just watch. Zara won't hurt you or anyone unless you try to get too close to him."

She spun away and ran to the edge, heart hammering against her ribs. Her lungs refused to work as she peered over.

"Sam," she yelled. Her vision was so dazzled by the brilliance of the arid landscape that she couldn't see him. Blinking hard, she looked again. Where was he? The slope was precariously steep, studded with rocks and juniper. If he'd tumbled all the way down, there was a jagged pile of boulders waiting at the bottom. He would be badly injured or worse. She heard Oliver's pleading voice. *Daddy...* Eyes burning, she scanned until tears ran down her face. There... Her heart jumped at the glimpse of blue.

Sam's blue T-shirt. She stared, trying to detect movement. *Lord, please let him be okay.* But he was completely still, as far as she could tell. Knocked unconscious? She would not allow herself to think the worst.

Edward edged in next to her, shoving a pair of binoculars into her hands. "Looks like that tree caught him, but he's not moving."

Through the lenses she could make out Sam's body, twisted and caught by the trunk of a sun-bleached tree. Was he moving? Alive? A silent prayer poured through her.

"I called for help," Ingrid said, breathless. "What happened? How could he possibly have fallen?"

At the moment, the only thing Daniella cared about was helping Sam. Cop training overrode the panic rising in her belly. *Come up with a plan and execute it.* A rescue team from the National Park Service would be en route but she had to render what first aid she could in the interim. The "golden hour," she knew, was the critical time after a traumatic injury in which treatment was most likely to make the difference between life and death.

Rope. There was a sturdy coil of climbing rope in the SUV, she'd noticed it earlier.

Daniella ran to the vehicle and yanked it out along with a small first aid kit she shoved into her waistband. Returning, she fastened a makeshift climbing harness and tied it off around a stone pillar.

"Are you sure this is safe?" Matthew asked. "Maybe one of the guys should…"

Her expression must have stopped the flow of his words because he didn't continue. Good thing for him.

"We'll steady you," Paul said as she tied the rope around her waist. Edward and Matthew took up positions to help.

Sweat was already running down her sides, her palms slippery. Were the men to be trusted? Probably not. But with so many witnesses, they wouldn't sabotage her efforts. Not like she had many other options. Time was speeding by and Sam lay in the heat, with who knew what injuries?

She looked over at Oliver, his face pale, fingers shoved in his mouth. Ingrid too was looking at the boy, perhaps intending to comfort him, but no one would get close with Zara there. The dog was rigid, eyes catching every movement, watching for anyone who might approach. If they did, Zara would follow her training and fight to her last breath to protect Oliver.

"Nanny Ella." Oliver's shrill voice carried over the sound of her own labored breaths.

His fear struck at her like a fist. She forced a smile

at him and a cheerful thumbs-up, but there was no time to reassure him. He'd started to cry harder, tears leaking down his face. Ingrid moved toward him, stopping abruptly when Zara let out a warning growl.

I'll get your daddy back, she silently promised Oliver. But in what condition? The fall had been a long one, the rocks interspersed with roots hardened into deadly spikes.

She'd get to Oliver's dad, no question, but would she find him alive? Gravely injured? Would she make things worse by trying to treat him? Yet how could she do anything else? The boy had already lost his mother. The thought of a life without Sam was intolerable. For a split second, she realized she was thinking about herself, not just Oliver.

Enough. Get moving.

After a silent prayer and one more quick look at Oliver, she walked herself backward over the wall and set off down the slope.

Sam's eyes flicked open to the blinding sun. His brain whirled as he tried to make sense of his situation. Pain radiated up his back and heat burned through his clothing.

The fall. He remembered. His brain told him to get to his feet, but his body would not cooperate. Terror swamped him. Had he been paralyzed? With all his effort, he managed to raise his head, sending a bolt of pain through his temples and, with it, relief that he could move a little. Oliver, he thought. How would he get to Oliver? But Daniella and Zara would be protecting his son, surely. The heat was so intense, he was having trouble forming a thought. His mouth was too sand-paper-dry for him to shout for help. He had the sensation of wood stabbing into his back, a branch or stump.

He tried again to get to his feet, but a trickle of grit spattered his face, indicating movement, coming from above. Maybe the cliff side was giving way. Was he about to be swept further down the slope? With effort, he turned his head and saw a desiccated branch thrust up next to him. Groaning, he hooked an arm around the protruding piece of wood. It was hot to the touch and seemed to transfer even more warmth into his body until he felt as if his blood was beginning to boil in his veins.

"Hold still," a voice said.

The light blinded him, but he knew that voice and his spirit leaped. "Daniella?" Her shadow crept over him, easing away the burning sun. He opened his eyes and, incredibly, there she was, those dark irises roving over him, a graceful smile on her lips. She was kneeling next to him, a rope fastened around her waist. "You... you came down here for me?"

She brushed some grit from his forehead. "Dumb question, Kavanaugh. Why else would I rappel down a cliff and lose my favorite baseball cap in the process? You owe me a new one, by the way." Her words were teasing and he would have smiled if he wasn't so worried. "Ollie," he croaked.

"Zara's got him and John's also watching. He's scared, but unhurt. You can give me the rundown about what happened after we get you out of here, okay?" She ran her hands deftly over his arms and legs and skimmed them along the back of his neck. "Doesn't feel like anything's displaced, but I'm no medic, so you shouldn't move until the park service rescue crew is on scene."

He watched, perplexed as she pulled off her jacket. After a few minutes, she'd managed to fasten the fabric over the tree branches. The shade it created was a profound relief. Then she activated a chemical ice pack from her kit and placed it on his forehead. Bliss. Pure and simple.

"Drink," she commanded, holding a silver package of emergency water to his lips. Some of it dribbled down his chin, but he sucked greedily, feeling as though he might never get enough.

"There now," she said. "Shade, water and company. What more could you want?"

He sighed. "Not a thing except to get back up to my son."

"Soon," she said. Her dark hair was damp with perspiration.

"I'm okay. I can climb up," he said after a fortifying breath. He tried to sit up.

"You're going to do nothing of the kind," she said firmly, holding him still with a palm on his chest. "And if you insist on moving, I'm going to have to handcuff you to this tree stump, which will really confuse the rescue team."

He would have laughed if it didn't hurt so much. She'd continued her exam, poking and patting. "I don't see any external bleeding, so we'll just stay still here for now, unless you do something inconvenient like stop breathing or go into shock or the like."

"I'll try not to."

"Good, because I'm a nanny, not a trauma nurse." She opened another pouch of water and trickled some in his mouth. It had to be the sweetest water he'd ever tasted, easing away the dust that coated his throat.

Removing the handkerchief she'd tied around her neck, she moistened it and bathed his face. Closing his eyes, he allowed himself to be comforted by the gentle pressure. She'd risked her own safety to rappel a cliff for him. It was beyond belief until he reminded himself that serving and protecting was her job. Yet her touch was so tender and filled with what seemed like deep fondness. In spite of his circumstances, he felt himself slipping into the twilight of sleep.

Above came the wail of a siren. She patted his chest. "They'll be here soon, Sam. Can you hear them?"

Everything was growing fuzzy in his mind. But there was something important, crucial, he needed to tell her.

"Stay awake," she said, and he thought he felt her lips on his forehead, the brush of her hair on his cheek. That surely must be part of his dream.

"I..." he said, but it came out no more than a whisper.

"What is it?" she said, putting her cheek to his lips. "Stay here, talk to me. Don't leave me, Sam, okay?" A tinge of pleading threaded through her strong voice.

He tried again, but the buzzing in his head was louder now, darkness nibbling at the edges of his consciousness. She smelled sweet; a combination of shampoo and sunshine. *Focus, Sam. Tell her.* But she was stroking the damp cloth on his face now, the cool water easing the burning from his skin, and his resolve was slipping slowly away.

Summoning all his strength, he reached out for her, his fingers grazing her hair. She leaned over, the dark pools of her eyes like spots of blessed shade in the scorched sky. He fought to form the words.

"Someone pushed me," he said.

And then his strength failed him, and he sank into unconsciousness.

Daniella dialed her boss from the hospital. Tyson had cleared the way for her to bring Zara into the facility. Oliver sat on a waiting room chair, crunching a bag of chips she'd bought for him from the vending machine. He offered one to Zara. Zara looked to Daniella with hope, but he would not eat unless she allowed it. With a smile, she gave permission for Zara to gulp the treat. Sam wouldn't want Oliver eating junk food either, but now was the time for gentleness not rules. The boy's face was still swollen from crying and he'd clung to Zara the entire way to the hospital.

"You okay?" Tyson asked as he picked up. "Rappelling without proper gear is risky."

"I didn't have any other choice except to wait for emergency," Daniella said.

He chuckled. "And waiting isn't your strong suit. Tell me again what Sam said."

"He told me he was pushed. It could have been any one of the guests."

"What's the doc's prognosis?"

"Only a mild concussion and bruised ribs, amazingly," she said with a gusty sigh. "Sam is one tough guy."

Tyson echoed her sigh with one of his own. "Happy to hear that."

"He'll have to stay in the hospital overnight, but possibly be released tomorrow, barring any complications. I've already talked to the local PD, so they know I'm working here and they'll protect my cover while they question the bystanders. They sent a patrol officer to check the lodge, and he didn't notice anything amiss."

"You're not surprised?"

"Not really. Whoever pushed him created the perfect diversion. They had loads of time to get a cab or bum a ride to the lodge and search uninterrupted while I was helping Sam. Mae was out shopping during that time so she wouldn't have seen anyone. John said all of them continued on with their hiking plans after the ambulance left but there's no way to verify that. Could be two of them, working together too, but…"

"But?"

"I assume that the assault was a way to get Sam off the property for a while, but that's the perplexing part. There is nothing of value here that would warrant it. Not that we can tell anyway. Hannah had collectibles, but none worth risking prison for. We don't know the who or the why."

"I'd wonder if Sam had kept something from us, if I didn't know him to be a straight arrow. I trust him."

"Me too." Daniella was surprised to find that she had grown to trust Sam Kavanaugh one hundred percent in the short time she'd been there. Not only did she believe he'd been completely honest about his circumstances, he'd been honest about his emotions. And that required massive courage, as far as she was concerned. He loved his son, struggled as a widower and a parent, and had deep misgivings about his own abilities, yet he persevered. His lion's heart made her own beat faster. An image of the three of them, her, Sam and Oliver, together, would not leave her mind. Troubling.

"Daniella?"

She realized she'd not heard Tyson's last remark.

"Oh, sorry. What did you say?"

"Figured while we were talking, I'd update you on a couple of things about the missing baby case."

Why did her work at the Rocky Mountain K-9 Unit seem so far away at the moment, with Sam in the hospital, her mind spinning with details about caring for Oliver?

"Kate Montgomery is officially awake and talking."

Daniella gasped. She was the only witness who could shed light on what had happened—who'd set her car on fire, since they knew it was deliberate. Why infant Chloe Baker's car seat and baby blanket had been found close by. What her connection was to Chloe's mother, who'd been found dead in her car in a ravine just miles from Kate's crime scene…

And the biggest question: where was baby Chloe?

Daniella clutched the phone. "Finally. What does she remember?"

"Nothing about who torched her car, unfortunately. Her head injury has caused short-term memory issues."

Daniella groaned.

"But her older memories are still intact," Tyson continued. "She does remember Nikki Baker and her baby Chloe, but no details yet, so we're hoping her recent recall will improve as she heals. Local PD questioned her about the Rolex found in Nikki's apartment, but she didn't know whom the initials on the back could refer to."

Someone had given Nikki a very expensive watch. S.M., Daniella thought. *Who are you, S.M.? And what is your involvement—if any—with the missing baby and a dead mother?* "Seems like we have more questions than answers," Daniella said. Just like here, she thought. As she watched Oliver, she realized her focus was entirely on Sam and the lodge.

You'll snap back into it when you return to Denver.

For some reason, the thought settled like a stone in the pit of her stomach.

"I'll keep you in the loop, and you do the same," Tyson said before he disconnected.

She was able to visit Sam briefly, but he was groggy and so tired he could barely keep his eyes open. She let Oliver have a short visit, long enough to reassure the boy. Her heart screamed at her to stay with Sam, but Oliver was tired and he needed a proper meal and his bed. It's what Sam would have insisted on, had he been more alert.

After making sure there was extra security at the door to Sam's room, she took Oliver back to the lodge, arriving in the late afternoon. Mae fixed Oliver a bowl of mac and cheese, which he gobbled.

Late that evening, while Mae read Oliver a story in his room, Zara watching over both of them, Daniella did her own cursory search of the property. The guests were occupied at the dinner table, discussing what had happened to Sam and their own hiking exploits. Nothing showed signs of being gone through; nothing was out of place. She'd questioned them as casually as she could manage about the incident, how close they'd been to Sam, hoping her interrogation came off as curiosity. She'd turned up nothing of note. Frustrated, she returned to Oliver's room and relieved Mae of duty.

Oliver had rolled onto his side. Eyes closed. Daniella heaved a sigh. He was asleep already. Perfect.

She recited the evening scripture to Zara, who curled up on the end of Oliver's mattress. Daniella had caved to Oliver who begged for Zara to sleep on the foot of his bed. Every once in a while, Oliver would stretch his toes down to make sure Zara was still there. Daniella sat in the rocker and tried to analyze her feelings. Never her strong suit. Frustration at not being able to pick out a culprit from the tiny group of five? Somewhat, but that came with cop territory. The job had become claustrophobic, so many cases solved, yes, but every crime left damage in its wake that was not correctable. It all pressed in on her.

A murdered woman, a baby snatched? A possible baby smuggling ring. The RMK9 Unit could solve the case, and they would, but they couldn't put the pieces of ruined lives back together. That darkness seemed to smother her sometimes, making her long for the wide-open spaces that she couldn't get to via a police car.

"Restless spirit," Uncle Cal would have said. She wanted to see Uncle Cal, to spend time with him in his older years and pour into him some of the love he'd infused into her.

The secret dream materialized in her mind again, a tiny cabin with room for Zara, a place to wake up and greet the morning without strapping on a weapon and facing the darkest humanity had to offer. A place near her uncle. For a while, she'd even thought she might be a foster parent someday too, but the few precious hours she'd spent with her own baby had taught her that parenting required a deep well of courage that she did not possess. It shamed her, that self-discovery. She turned her mind back to her daydreams.

Just her and Zara in a wilderness somewhere. Sunshine, guiding groups to see the wonders God had made, instead of the evil humans had wrought. It would fill the restless void inside her, she was sure of it.

A whimper jerked her from her musings. Oliver was sitting up, lower lip trembling.

What should I do? She tried to quell her jitters. He was a boy, not the boogeyman. "Uh, hey, Oliver. I'm right here. You're not alone."

Would that do the trick? He continued to whimper in spite of Zara's immediate tongue swabbing. Daniella pushed Zara back and sat next to Oliver.

"Do you need to go potty? Or… I mean if you had an accident, that's okay. I know where Daddy keeps your dinosaur underwear. I can get you a pair, no sweat." Potty? Dinosaur underwear? What would her colleagues think about her now? Oliver's soft sobs turned into shuddering gulps. Wet pants weren't the cause of the outburst, then. She didn't blame him for being upset after what he'd experienced.

What else soothed kids? "How about a snack? I can go get you something." Sam wouldn't want him to have cookies, but maybe crackers. She'd put some on a plate with some juice. No, not juice. That was bad at night, wasn't it? Milk? But then, would he need to brush his teeth again after the eating and drinking? And probably delivering fluids would have consequences later on, wouldn't it?

Her frantic thoughts died away as Oliver looked at her. It was as if his heart cracked wide open. Tears rolled down his face. "Daddddeeeeeee," he wailed. Daddy. He wanted his father. Or maybe his subconscious longed for Hannah too, a mother he hadn't known but still felt the absence of. Zara howled softly, as if she also understood the depth of Oliver's sadness.

For a moment, Daniella was immobilized and then, somehow, she was folding him into her arms, pressing her cheek against his head. "It's okay. Daddy is okay. He's going to come home tomorrow. Let's practice our signs for 'safe,' okay?"

But Oliver continued to wail, so she scooped him up and walked around the room singing the only song she could think of. "Jingle Bells."

Smooth, Daniella. "Jingle Bells" in July. When his father's in the hospital and his mother's dead and someone is terrorizing him. This dearth of maternalism was why she'd known she'd had to give her own child away and should not have any more. Maybe it was imprinted from her own mother, the lack of a loving woman in her life. Daniella's daughter was an emerging preteen now, and she had a good life with a solid family, Daniella reminded herself. But that was because she had amazing adoptive parents who knew what to do. With this sobbing child, Daniella had nothing to offer but a sad-sack rendition of "Jingle Bells" to ease his terror.

Zara paced around behind her as she trudged along. It took almost one entire circuit of the room before she noticed that Oliver was not sobbing anymore. He'd pressed his wet face to her neck and begun to hum along.

Incredulous, she kept on singing, toggling him against her as they traveled until finally, at long last, she felt the regular breathing of a sleeping child. She did another few laps, afraid to stop, until Zara nosed the mattress, staring at her as if to say, "He needs to go back to bed now."

"You think he's really out?" she whispered to Zara.

The dog stamped two front paws on the mattress, the message unmistakable. Put. Him. Down.

"Okay," she murmured, "but if you're wrong, you get to listen to another dozen choruses of 'Jingle Bells.'"

Easing Oliver onto the bed did not wake him and she was able to pull the covers up as Zara resettled herself. Midnight the cat turned around from his spot on the high shelf and closed his eyes too.

For a long moment, Daniella stared at the sleeping boy. She could not quite sort out her jumble of emotions. Was it satisfaction she felt? Triumph? Tenderness? Or something deeper that stirred in the place her own mother had left vacant?

She resumed her spot in the rocking chair and let the soft creaking keep rhythm to her prayers…for Sam, for Oliver, and her own expression of gratitude.

Oliver's soul was comforted…and she'd played a part in that.

It felt better than solving any case in her entire career.

A certainty crept into her heart. She'd been brought here by the Lord to protect this child and his father, and maybe to learn a few lessons about herself along the way.

Smiling, she rocked in silence as she watched over Sam's little boy.

NINE

Sam's fingers still gripped his cell phone, the screen clicked off now. The hospital sheets were twisted around his legs. He could not erase what he'd seen on the baby monitor app. Daniella soothing Oliver, calming him to sleep. A soft song, the slow laps around the tiny bedroom.

Mothering him, his soul chided.

"Well what did you want her to do? Let Oliver cry himself to sleep?" he muttered to himself.

No, of course he didn't. But he also didn't want his son getting the wrong message. Daniella was not his mother.

Sam knew his own reaction didn't make sense. She'd done the right thing. Nonetheless, his heart hammered with agitation.

Oliver was young, and hungry for a mother figure. He'd get confused.

His head pounded and sweat beaded his forehead as his thoughts chased one another through his skull.

He'll forget Hannah. He'll forget his mother.

He tried to calm himself with a prayer, but still his pulse revved to uncomfortable levels like he'd experienced after his return to civilian life. The sensations of war were buried deep in his memory. He could recall with painful vividness the heat of the stifling Humvee, the sweat that coated them all as they'd wondered if the radio frequency jammers would disrupt the device they'd discovered in the road long enough for them to neutralize it.

One moment in time was permanently etched into him: the deafening blast on that sizzling day that took the legs of his buddy on the last month of his tour. Blinking hard, Sam put the memories back into the box where he kept them. He was here, at the hospital, and the threat was not some explosive device but a living, breathing, person. He was probably just upset because of his interaction with Daniella.

Part of his brain informed him he was being completely nonsensical. Hannah was Oliver's mother and no one could erase that simply by helping to care for him. So why did it feel like he was betraying her by letting Daniella step up? And why was his own heart opening to Daniella in spite of his fears?

When he got home, he'd show Oliver the videos of his first few weeks, with Hannah crooning and laughing. And the stuffed animal she'd given him that he no longer wanted to sleep with. What else could he do or try? Suddenly he felt utterly exhausted. Was that the role God meant for him? To spend the years in constant struggle to keep Hannah alive in Oliver's world? To be the history keeper? The memory maker? To push away other people who could provide comfort for his son... and himself?

That last bit twisted a knife in his gut. He remembered the tenderness of Daniella's touch as she'd shielded him from the sun, putting her own life at risk to preserve his. An echo of that feeling still buzzed through his nerves. He shifted, the smell of hospital disinfectant stinging his nostrils and the bland-painted walls closing in on him. He did enjoy being near her, and he found her presence comforting. More than comforting. That was the truth, whether he wanted to admit it or not.

He kicked the blanket into a rumpled pile. Of course, why wouldn't he enjoy having Daniella close? Totally natural. She was doing her job, protecting him and his son. But deep down, he worried that his feelings for her did not stem entirely from her cop identity. She was interesting, intelligent, fearless; her abruptness so different from Hannah. They were similar in some ways also. Hannah had fought cancer with a ruthless resolve. He remembered the agonized moment when he'd had to make her see the fearful truth that the treatments were not working.

Hannah, you're sick, very sick. You can't ignore it or will it away. We...we need to make a plan about how to handle this. His heart had cracked a little more with each word he'd spoken.

It was the look she'd given him then, the question nestled deep in her lovely green eyes that would stay with him forever. *I'm not going to make it, am I?* she'd said.

He'd said the only thing he could. "I love you," grabbing up her ravaged frame and pulling her close, praying the tests were wrong, the X-rays, the blood results, everything.

But the doctors had known before he and Hannah had come to terms with it. She wasn't going to defeat the cancer, no matter how hard she fought, nor how much she loved Oliver and him. All the sleepless nights, agonizing pain, the depletion of her body had come to nothing.

And she'd ended their conversation with one last phrase. *I want whatever's best for Oliver.*

Jaw tight, he looked at the monitor app on his cell phone again, Oliver sleeping soundly, Zara a furry ball at his feet. He could not see Daniella, except the tiny shadow cast by the rocking chair indicated she stood sentry, protecting his son.

His son. Now was not the time to be stewing over his relationship with Daniella or grieving the loss of Hannah. He'd nearly been killed the day before and the person who'd shoved him could be strolling around his lodge. While he lingered in this hospital bed, someone might be searching, making plans to burn it down to get what they wanted, to take it by force. Daniella would do her best to keep his son safe, but ultimately that responsibility was his and his alone.

Common sense trickled in. He was also injured and a civilian. Stalkers and intruders were best left to the people trained to deal with them. He checked the phone camera again. His son was fine, he told himself.

Another hour ticked away as he wrestled with what to do. Oliver, Daniella, Mae, the lodge, the guests, his whole world…

When he could stand it no longer, he summoned the night nurse. "I'm checking myself out," he said.

"Sir—" she started.

He held up a palm. "I'll sign whatever you want me to. I know it's not what the doctor ordered. My son needs me."

"All right," she said with a sigh. "I'll start the paperwork."

Then it was a matter of finding his clothes and waiting for another hour until he was almost ready to walk out, paperwork or not. The frenzied feeling bubbled up as he scribbled his name on the papers and waited for the Uber he'd arranged to take him home.

His primary goal thrummed through him again and again. *I have to keep things the same for Oliver.*

He made it to the lodge before the sun rose, climbing out headachey and slightly nauseous.

Daniella greeted him in the kitchen. Of course she'd known he was coming, the three cameras would have made sure of that.

She folded her arms. "What do you think you're doing? You were supposed to be discharged at noon, if you were cleared by the doctor, that is."

"I cleared myself," he said. "I'm fine. Did you find out anything about who shoved me over?" He heard the tone in his voice, brusque, almost confrontational. What was he doing?

"No," she said cautiously. "I didn't, though I pressed the guests as much as I could. And there wasn't anything disturbed here at the lodge that I could tell."

"Okay. I want to see my son. Thanks for putting him to bed when he was upset. I saw it on the camera." He turned to go.

"Is that what's bothering you?" She looked half annoyed and half uncertain. "The way I handled that with Oliver?"

"No, of course not. You were great. I want to see him, that's all." But she was right. It was exactly the reason for his angst. She'd handled the situation like a mother.

Oliver's mother.

She stopped him, her expression flat and detached, as it had been when she'd first arrived. "All right. Let me go first and get Zara. We'll leave you alone for a while. If you want to sleep with him tonight, we'll sack out on the sofa in the library. We can hear any trouble from there."

"You don't need to…"

"Obviously, I do."

He knew he had not concealed his true feelings from her, not for one moment. She could read his emotions as easily as she deciphered Zara's. *You're a jerk, Sam. And she doesn't deserve how you're treating her.* He had no idea how to fix things between them, or even if he should. Detachment was better, wasn't it?

She pushed the hair off her brow. "John will be here at 7:30 a.m. to take the guests to the cliff dwelling hike," she said coolly. "Mae is making crepes at six thirty, if you wanted to know that. You can sleep in since everything's handled."

"Sure," he said, forcing himself to look at her. "I… I really do appreciate you taking care of Oliver. It's just…"

"That I'm not his mother." She cocked her head, giving him a full-on stare. "You know what? I already know that. And I'm also clear that no one is ever going to step into that role, especially me. News flash, Sam. I don't want to be a mother. I had a shot at that, and I gave it up. I'm not here to replace Hannah. I'm leaving as soon as we wrap up the case." She turned and headed for the stairs. "Enjoy your family time."

"Daniella…" But she was already gone. Why had he treated her rudely when she'd done nothing but help?

...no one is ever going to step into that role.

It sounded final, harsh. But isn't that what he wanted? What was right for Oliver? It must be best to make sure no one crowded Oliver's mother out of his memories. And to keep everyone far away from Hannah's place in his own heart.

Is that what he was really doing? Guaranteeing, with his behavior, that no one would ever be a mother to Oliver? That he would live his whole life with an empty place where Hannah should have been?

I don't want to be a mother. I had a shot at that and I gave it up.

But she would be a fantastic mother if she allowed herself the opportunity. Did God want her to find that with Oliver?

Uncertainty gnawed at him.

What am I doing, Lord? Help me figure this out before it's too late for Oliver.

*And for me...*his heart added.

Daniella retrieved Zara, who wasn't thrilled about leaving Oliver's side. They padded down to the kitchen for a drink of water. She figured it would be a quiet place to gather herself before the lodge would begin to stir. She wished she could call Jodie, but it was not yet 5:30 a.m. Besides, she was not sure she'd be able to explain her emotional jumble anyway.

The elation she'd experienced at soothing Oliver.

The anger she felt at Sam for resenting her actions.

And the hurt...

That part was a puzzle. She wasn't a person to stick around to be hurt and usually she didn't get close enough to anybody to give them the chance. There was no reason to care about Sam and his quest to keep Oliver away from real life. Not her problem.

But it did hurt, ached in fact, that Sam thought she was intruding on his family. He'd pushed her firmly back into the outsider's camp.

I don't want you here, his actions had said, *and my son is better off without you.*

That last thought brought tears, which she blinked away. Another child better off without her. The letters she received from Hope's adopted mother came with a series of photos…preschool and kindergarten, Hope graduating from elementary school, starting middle school wearing a "P-town Panthers" T-shirt, her grin still wide and warm.

Better off without you…

Message received, she told herself angrily. The sooner the case was closed, the better.

She was dismayed to find Whitney, Matt and Paul in comfortable chairs in the living room.

Paul waved at her. "You couldn't sleep either? I think it's the heat. Even with air-conditioning, you know it's a furnace out there waiting to incinerate you."

Then why visit the desert? she wanted to ask.

They were sipping glasses of ice water and, on the small table, there was a plate of oatmeal-raisin cookies remaining from the night before. He gestured for her to join them.

Why not? Maybe she could pick up a previously unmentioned detail that might help her leave this lodge behind more quickly.

"We were talking about what happened to Sam," Whitney said. Her long hair was twisted into a knot on the top of her head. "He didn't fall over by himself, did he? He had to have been pushed."

Daniella reminded herself she was a nanny, not a closemouthed cop. "I think so too, but who would have reason to do that? Sam's just an innkeeper, not a guy with enemies."

"He must have someone out to get him, maybe even someone he thinks of as a friend." Paul considered the cookie he'd selected from the plate. "You never know about people. I worked with an ex-con in my shipping business for three years and didn't know it."

"Why is that a problem?" Matt demanded, brows drawn in an angry line. "Did the guy mess with you? Steal from you?"

Paul blinked. "No. Just pointing out that people can be many things, as my dad used to say."

Matt snorted. "That's right, and people make mistakes. You ever make a mistake? Done something you weren't proud of?"

Paul offered a breezy smile. "I don't have an over-abundance of guilt in my life. That's counterproductive, but I see I've hit a sore spot with you, Matt."

"I'm an ex-con," Matt said, "and I'd never shove someone over a wall."

Whitney straightened. "He went to jail for assault, but it was a misunderstanding. That's all."

"I don't need you to defend me, Whit." He surged out of his chair. "I'm going for a walk."

Whitney watched him uncertainly. "It's a sensitive point with Matt, of course. He's grown and changed a lot since he was arrested. He'd never hurt anyone now. I'd better go talk to him. See you later."

Paul watched her depart. "Wow. I didn't see that coming, did you?"

"No," Daniella said, wondering why Jodie's search hadn't turned up the info. *But I'm going to find out about that misunderstanding.* "I guess people have all kinds of stories they keep under wraps." She pretended to scan the photos above the mantel, Zara watching her every move.

"So your sister knew Sam's wife Hannah when they were in college?"

He nodded. "Uh-huh. Besties is the term, though I think Ingrid felt betrayed when Sam came along and swept Hannah off her feet. The dashing soldier and all that. My sister's the type who wants all of a person. Obsessive, you know? She's done her best to smother me over the years. Feels like it's her duty or something since I'm the baby." He shrugged. "I've run three different businesses and started a law degree, but she still wants to manage my life. It's exhausting, really. She never takes the easy way out of anything."

"Three businesses? Impressive. What type?"

His smile was wide. "A little of this and that. I'm a restless soul. Haven't found what I want to stick with, you know?"

Like whether to stay in law enforcement or act out her daydreams of wilderness exploration? "I can relate."

"Nanny isn't your lifelong goal?"

"No." The conversation was getting to be too much about her, and she needed to get away from any prying questions. She had enough to go on. Law school, three businesses. His sister Ingrid perhaps dangerously attached to Hannah. Might the attacks be a way to punish Sam for taking Hannah to the States? Perhaps Paul was wrong about Ingrid's motives. It was possible that Ingrid had resented Hannah because she had feelings for Sam.

The dashing soldier and all that.

A cocky businessman.

A potentially jealous sister.

Matt with his history of assault. She had plenty to digest.

Paul yawned. "Guess I'll snooze for another hour or so until kickoff time. See you later."

Whitney and Matt had not returned. "Want to take a quick walk outside, Zara?"

The Malinois's tail wagged as if to say, "Is a walk ever a bad idea?"

They eased out the kitchen door. The pre-dawn temperatures were not cool, but deliciously moderate compared to the sizzling daytime. A scent hung in the air, the strange aroma of distant moisture, and she remembered Sam had talked about a summer storm system. Rain in this parched and thirsty season would be a welcome blessing.

She and Zara circled the patio without seeing Matthew or Whitney. Might they have walked to the rear entrance? She checked the camera app on her phone. Wherever they'd gotten to, they were not in camera range.

The mournful howl of a coyote pricked Zara's ears. The sound made the hairs on Daniella's arms stand on end. It felt as if it held an urgent warning of approaching danger. All kinds of covert activity in the vast Gila Wilderness. She lingered a few more minutes, but there was still no sign of Whitney, Matt or anyone else.

Zara went taut, nose quivering.

"What is it, girl?"

The dog was facing the main house, which appeared to be dark and quiet at first glance. Maybe there had been a fox or rat slinking along the periphery? Zara's laser focus continued. Daniella finally noticed the very small window set low down, almost at ground level. It must allow in light for a basement, or lower level storage area, one that Sam hadn't told her about.

She did not understand the reason for Zara's attention until a gleam flickered across the window and then disappeared. Someone was in that room, someone who did not want to risk turning on a light, so they were using a flashlight or cell phone to help them.

Searching?

At long last, her moment had come.

Daniella called softly to Zara. "Let's go catch ourselves a bad guy, why don't we?"

TEN

Sam hugged his sleepy boy to his chest as tightly as he dared. The warmth, the heft of him, comforted Sam's soul enough for him to forget his pounding headache. "Thirsty," Oliver mumbled.

"We'll go get some water."

"Juice?"

Sam smiled. Not too sleepy to test his father's resolve. "Water," Sam said firmly.

"Snack?"

"All right," Sam said. "But no sugar. It's almost breakfast time."

The negotiations concluded, Sam carried Oliver out of his room past the library. He wanted to see Daniella, but he trained his gaze away from the door that was partly open, not wanting her to think he was being nosy. The way he'd left things still churned uncomfortably.

He padded into the kitchen, finding the half-eaten plate of cookies from some guest snackers. Before Oliver could snag one, he whisked them out of reach. Daniella entered abruptly from the outside, Zara primed and alert.

He tensed. "What…?"

She put a finger to her lips. "There's a lower level room," she whispered. "Where?"

"You mean the basement?"

"No," she said with a tinge of impatience. "Something else. Through a small window, Zara saw someone sneaking around."

"But there's no—" His mouth closed with a snap. "Not a room, a crawl space. We converted part of it to storage after we had water damage in the old lodge. I forgot all about it." *Clod*, he chided himself. How could he have forgotten with so much at stake?

"Where's the access?"

He guided her to a broom closet in the corner next to the refrigerator. "Trapdoor in the floor." He wanted to say all kinds of silly things about how he should check it first, and maybe she should watch Oliver. Laughable, since he was not the trained professional. He'd have to put the kibosh on his protective instincts. He didn't have the right to push her away and insert himself as her backup.

She didn't wait for his comments anyway. Pulling open the door, she and Zara vanished inside. He moved Oliver away into the living room and sat him down with his snack. "I'll be standing right there while you eat, okay?"

Oliver's eyes widened but he nodded, munching away on his cracker.

Grabbing a frying pan in one hand and trying to look nonchalant about it, Sam readied his cell in the other and stationed himself in the threshold between the two rooms. If anything went bad, or Daniella flushed out the intruder, Sam intended to stop them in their tracks before they left the kitchen. They would not reach his son in the living room. That was dead certain. He would do what he could to help Daniella whether he had a right to or not.

Thinking of her trapped in that contained space with an intruder made his fingers ice over. What was it like to be married to a spouse who performed such a dangerous job? Spouse? Why had that thought crowded in?

"Pay attention," he commanded himself.

Footsteps distracted him and he whirled to find Mae coming through the kitchen door, a bag of groceries cradled to her hip. She started when she saw him. "I…"

He held a finger to his lips and pointed to the trap door.

She sidled over on tiptoe. "I came early to work on the crepes," she whispered. "What's going on?"

"Tell you later. Can you take Oliver back to his room and stay with him for a few minutes?"

She caught sight of Oliver eating his snack in the living room and gave Sam a thumbs-up. The worried pucker on her lips was concealed behind a bright smile for the boy as she took his hand and led him toward the stairs.

At least his son was well out of the danger range. Now if only Daniella would be okay… He crept a little closer, just as Zara's ears appeared in the trap door. "We gotta work on your ladder skills," Daniella grunted as she helped Zara clear the rungs and then climbed out behind her. Her hair was mussed, cheeks flushed.

"Whoever was down there busted through a ventilation screen to get in and out. What's in those boxes?"

He tried to recall. "I didn't remember there was anything left at all, to be honest. I thought we'd gradually cleared it all out over the years."

"You didn't. One box was open, as if it had been searched. Looks like old books, mostly."

"More of my wife's things. She had so many belongings when she moved from Germany, we had a whole room at the old lodge crammed. She gradually whittled her stash down, but there was quite a bit left when the water pipe burst, so we moved the things here. I'm sorry I forgot about that. But I don't see the relevance anyway. As I told you, there's nothing valuable in Hannah's collection."

"Somebody thinks there is."

Sam considered. "Well that somebody had to be an acquaintance, right? Ingrid had ties to Hannah in Germany. They were roommates. Do you think she decided Hannah had something worth taking?"

"Could be. Did Hannah know Paul?"

"She never mentioned him and I didn't meet him when I visited."

"We need to go through the boxes right now," Daniella said. "Quickly, before the guests awaken."

"Oliver's upstairs with Mae," Sam said uneasily.

"I'll take Zara up, and she'll watch too." Daniella jogged off to deliver Zara to her assignment.

Sam didn't want to acknowledge the surge of relief he felt that Zara would keep Oliver safe. Hopefully their search would be over quickly, allowing Mae to attend to her duties. Trouble or not, the lodge had to keep running if he was going to make the payments. Every nickel was tied up in the Cliffside and there was no backup plan. The guests needed to get their money's worth or they'd tank him with uncomplimentary reviews. The promised crepe breakfast and cliff tour would have to move forward, regardless of the circumstances. At least John

could handle the transportation so Sam could catch up
on his lodge chores, nasty ones like paying bills and
having the finicky air conditioner serviced.

Daniella rejoined him. Clutching two flashlights
she'd retrieved, they descended the ladder into the musty
crawl space. He'd not taken the time to do much more
than lay a sheet of plywood over the hard-packed earth
and a plastic tarp between the wood and the boxes to
protect from any moisture. The small space put him in
close proximity to Daniella. So close, her hair brushed
his cheek and he could feel the warmth of her body.

He wanted to apologize, to move closer, to try to explain why he'd treated her badly, yet no words would
come. She let her gaze linger on his for a moment before she reached to undo the flaps on the nearest box.
His breath hitched. Let this be the answer, he prayed.

Daniella held up a sweater, one of the thick handmade ones Hannah's aunt had knitted for her. The box
was crammed with them in the rich jewel colors that
Hannah preferred. He fingered the green one, soft as a
cloud, that had been her favorite. It should have been
excruciating to see those garments there, but instead
it awakened only a low-grade sadness. Was he too allowing Hannah to slip from his heart? He hadn't even
remembered the boxes still piled beneath the inn. Another piece of her packed away.

Forgotten, his heart accused.

Daniella was already on to the next box. She pulled out
an empty glass globe and shot him a questioning look.

"Snow globes. Hannah loved them. Some sort of
fascination with them since she lived in the desert as a
kid, I think. Anyway, she had a bunch like the ones in
the library, but this one broke when Midnight knocked

it off the mantel. I should have thrown it away, I guess, but I salvaged the pieces as best I could." That was a metaphor for life: a salvage operation.

"Are there more anywhere else?"

"No. I moved the survivors off the mantel after the cat incident. There are only three left, in the library, locked in a glass case that you've already seen. But I bought one of them for her myself and I can tell you, it's not worth anything to anyone. I spent maybe thirty bucks on it. The two others she got from her relatives, I think."

"Let's go look at them anyway. If these threats have roots in the past, there might be a link."

"Look now?"

"What's more important?" She was all business, a clear message hidden in the words. *We're not friends... or anything else. I'm here to do a job.*

He heaved out a breath. "What's more important is that I apologize to you for my behavior. You did nothing wrong. As a matter of fact, you were brilliant with Oliver. Hannah..." He cleared his throat. "Hannah would have wanted him to be comforted and she would have been full of gratitude, which is how I should've behaved. I'm sorry."

Her eyes gleamed black in the gloom, the slight cock of her chin indicating she was deep in thought. "But it felt weird to have someone else mothering him. It felt weird to be doing it, honestly. I'm not wired that way." She waved a hand. "Not much maternal instinct."

"Even more reason for me to ask for your forgiveness. You went out on a limb. Pushed yourself because you wanted to help Ollie."

"And you." She shrugged, as if she were suddenly

embarrassed by her admission. "I care about you both, is what I meant."

She cared about him too? It thrilled him to hear it. Daniella did not have a large circle of people she allowed herself to care about, he thought. Blessed, he figured, to be one of them. "Thank you, Daniella. It's what I should have said right from the beginning. Thank you."

She looked back at him before wrapping her arms around her torso. "I accept your apology. I can see why you're struggling."

He thought about her odd comment. *I don't want to be a mother. I had a shot at that and I gave it up.*

"You said earlier that you'd had a chance at being a mom," he said gently. "What did you mean by that?"

"My teen years were a mess. I had a baby at sixteen. A girl." She pulled in a breath and let it out slowly. "My daughter won't know me either, not really. Even though that was my choice to give her up, it hurts sometimes."

He pointed to her gold charm. "Is that a memento?" he asked softly.

She touched it, fingers buffing the gold. "It's her fingerprint, a gift from her adoptive family. She was only a few hours' old when I gave her to them. It was the best choice. The right choice."

"A courageous choice."

"Yes. I knew I wouldn't give her what she deserved, I was a junior in high school when I became pregnant. I had no job. Uncle Cal found me living under the bleachers behind the football field. He's not my uncle by blood, but I call him that. He took me in, got me to the doctor, saw that I earned my GED. He helped me with the adoption arrangements." Daniella sighed. "She was beautiful. Still is, she's thirteen now. I get pictures sometimes."

He did not want to stop the flow of tender words. "What is her name?"

Daniella's smile was soft. "They let me name her. I chose Hope."

"Beautiful." He smiled too, and the moment stretched between them like a cooling breeze. He savored the gift he had been given to understand her, to know her more deeply. "Thank you for telling me about Hope."

Daniella nodded. "Don't know why I did, but something about you makes me spill my guts."

He laughed. "My rugged good looks and manly, boy-next-door charm?"

"Nah," she said. "That's not it."

His chuckled turned into a full-on guffaw. "No doubt."

"Getting late," she said, checking her cell phone. "Can you unlock the library cases?"

"Yes, ma'am," he said as they headed for the ladder. Though he didn't see why, he felt lighter, less burdened than he had ten minutes before. He did not think the snow globes would shed any light whatsoever, but at least he'd been given the gift of peeking into Daniella's heart and the grace of being forgiven.

And she'd said she cared for both him and his son.

That was a win he would hang on to.

Daniella knew she should feel awkward at having divulged so much to Sam. She'd actually told him about Hope. That was something she hadn't even shared with Jodie or anyone else. For some reason, the admission left her more relaxed than she'd thought possible. Relaxed was *not* the way she should be feeling.

Would ya get your head back to the case?

She realized Sam had already gotten to the library door before her and she scrambled to catch up. He was thumbing through a ring of keys as he entered and approached the display case. Since they'd never found the missing master key, Sam had a copy made of the last remaining one and he no longer hung it on the peg in the kitchen. The lower shelves were completely blocked by the small sofa placed in front of it, the one that Daniella had decided to sleep on for the night. Even she hadn't noticed there were lower shelves concealed by the furniture.

Excellent. If she hadn't noticed, then the person who was sneaking around the inn likely hadn't either. They were about due for a break in their favor.

Sam grabbed the arm of the sofa and began to scoot it out of the way.

"I'll close the door," she said, but she turned to find Edward Reese standing on the threshold, staring. She tried to cover her dismay with an easy smile.

"Hi," she said.

Sam stopped moving the sofa immediately. "Hello, Edward. What can I do for you?"

Edward's eyes narrowed. "I was on my way to breakfast. Heard you in here. Moving furniture?"

Sam nodded. "Always something to do around here. Dust bunnies everywhere."

"But you didn't bring a vacuum to clean underneath?" Edward asked.

"Uh, no," Sam said.

Daniella was about to jump in and smooth things over when Edward looked around her.

"Hey, I never noticed there were display shelves down there."

Daniella muttered to herself. Why did Edward have to be so observant?

He took a step closer. "Need some help?"

"No, thank you," Sam said. "I should get in there and dust. It's a one-man job, but thanks."

Edward didn't move. "My dad ran a jewelry store in Germany his whole life. My job as a young man was dusting shelves. Man, I hated that job. Eighteen-year-old with better things to do earning minimum wage. Dad wasn't one to go for coddling so I moved away the moment I was old enough." His gaze wandered from Daniella to Sam and the display case behind him. "Now I know those were the good days, working with Dad, helping out instead of frittering away my time and money."

"Does your father still run his store?" Sam asked.

Edward shook his head. "It was robbed one night about four years ago. He took a big loss, and the stress gave him a heart attack. He can barely walk now, and he's in a wheelchair."

"I'm sorry," Sam said.

"Were the people caught?" Daniella asked. "The ones who robbed the store?"

"No." Edward seemed to have drifted to another place and time.

An inside job? Daniella wondered at the guilt she saw in Edward's expression. Guilt that he hadn't been there to help his father? She had a sudden thought. Perhaps it was guilt because he'd been part of the plan to steal from his dad? He wouldn't be the first son to betray his father.

"Funny that Ingrid and Paul lived in Germany too. I don't suppose you knew them?" she asked.

Edward shrugged. "No. Germany's a big place."

"Did you take over the family business?" Sam said. "I never did catch your profession."

"Nah. I'm not the personality type to run a small business. You gotta give your whole life to something like that. I went into insurance." He jutted his chin. "Sure you don't need some help?"

"No, thank you. It's almost time for breakfast anyway."

"Yeah, strawberry crepes," Edward said, his grin back in place. "I'm thinking of checking in here permanently, the food's so good."

He left and Daniella hastened to close the door.

"What did you make of that?" Sam said.

"Strikes me as unusual that three of the guests have a connection to Germany. I'll check the jewelry store thing."

"Your cop mind is running rampant, I can tell. You think the lodge stalker problem is related to jewelry?"

"Just considering that maybe we've got a heist gone bad here. Stolen jewelry that somehow wound up in the wrong place, where the thieves couldn't get their hands on it."

Sam reached for the little key and stared at it. "Jewelry, huh?"

"There's a much better market for jewelry than snow globes," Daniella said. "Easy to fence, and—" she helped him scoot the sofa out of the way "—easy to conceal inside something."

"Like a snow globe?"

"Let's find out," she said, her stomach tight with eagerness. Jewelry, she thought. Might that be what someone was so anxious to find? And what if it had been right under their noses the whole time?

ELEVEN

Sam unlocked the case and slid the glass shelf open while she shut the library door. The three snow globes occupied their respective spots, relatively free from dust. Two were Christmas themed, festooned outside and in with branches of holly and gaudy red bows. He handed the first to Daniella, who looked at the snowy village inside. The swirling flakes danced before her eyes.

Carefully, she turned it over and around, examining the globe from all sides. Sam was close, very close, staring into the pretend snow. Her nerves fluttered at the brush of his muscled arm against hers. Nerves? Why? Instead of forcing herself to analyze her reaction, she edged away a fraction, breaking their connection. Odd, how her heart whispered an objection. "Nowhere to hide anything in this one," she said.

He nodded. "That's what I was thinking. Snow globes just don't encompass a lot of square footage. Maybe we're wrong about the hidden gems notion. Would have been really fantastic though. Just like some sort of movie, hidden gems in a remote lodge."

"Due diligence," she said. "We check them all." She set the first one down as he offered her the next.

The tiny scene inside was a towering pine decorated with yellow birds and holly berries. Crystals glinted off the frosted top. Sparkly and intricate, definitely not Daniella's taste. This one was different because the pedestal underneath held a music box. She wound the knob and a Christmas carol played. When it finished, she peeked into the compartment with the mechanism. Nothing unusual. "Fancy, but not exactly the hidden treasure we were looking for."

He was reaching for the last snow globe, a valentine-themed one, when there was a jiggle on the door handle and Whitney and Matt came in.

"Oh, sorry. Are we interrupting?" Whitney said.

"No." Sam smoothly slid the door closed and locked it. Daniella tried to position herself to block their view of the cabinet, but there was too much of it to hide.

Matt quirked a brow. "Keeping your collectibles under lock and key?"

Whitney squeezed his arm in a playful way, but he did not smile. "Sure, Matt. Why wouldn't he?"

Matt shot a look at Daniella and then back to Sam. "Showing the nanny where you keep the treasures?"

Daniella beamed a smile at him. "Nah. I was passing by and I figured he could use help moving the sofa."

Matt didn't smile back. "That's above and beyond the call of duty for a nanny."

There was a challenge in the statement. Did he suspect she wasn't a nanny? Maybe her rappelling adventure had sparked his curiosity. There was definitely something simmering there.

"Come on, Matt," Whitney said, tugging him to the door. "I'm starved."

"Didn't you come in for a book?" Daniella asked.

Matt shook his head. "Changed my mind," he said before opening the door and stepping out, his wife following.

Sam looked thoughtful. "He's got an attitude, doesn't he?"

She realized she hadn't had a chance to tell him what Matt and Ingrid had revealed—that Matt had a record for assault and was touchy about it. She replayed the conversation. "I had our office assistant run some particulars. The reason we didn't know about his arrest record was that his name is actually Matthison, not Matthew. Happened when he was eighteen, an argument between friends about money that got out of hand. He did his time, ten months, and hasn't had a problem since."

A muffled bang jerked their attention.

"That came from my room," Sam said.

Daniella raced out of the library and into the hallway. She tried to shove open the door to his room and her shoulder met resistance. "Locked."

He moved her aside and unlocked it, trying to get in ahead of her, but she wouldn't allow it. Staying low, she flung the door open just as a heavy lamp with a clay base was thrown from across the room. Staggering back, she tripped on Sam's legs and stumbled to her knees with no time to deflect the heavy lamp. Sam shot out an arm and caught it inches before it impacted her skull. Breathing hard, Daniella scrambled to her feet.

The thrown lamp had allowed whoever had launched it to run through the adjoining room, the unoccupied guest suite. She careened in to find the space empty. Biting back a frustrated howl, she raced into the hallway, scanning in both directions. There was no one nearby. Trotting to the top of the stairs, she could not see any guests from that vantage point. Sam met her there.

"I checked the stairwell. Nothing." His frustration was evident in his clenched jaw, fingers curled into fists.

They returned to Sam's room. The drawers had been opened and rummaged. The same with the closet.

"If whoever this is was looking for valuables in here, they're misled. The only thing I've got that's worth anything is a bunch of clothes. Everything's old right down to my socks."

"Probably no prints either," she grumbled.

He set the lamp back in its place on the dresser.

"Thank you," she said. "For snagging that lamp before it cracked my skull open."

"You're welcome," he said without a smile. "I don't like how close it came."

"Me neither." She tried to joke but the concern in his eyes warmed her.

He held up his hand, almost as if he would brush away the hair from her temple.

A bell jingled from downstairs and he sighed. "I have to pitch in for the breakfast service."

"Yes, right." She should be happy to be rescued from her silly reaction to his proximity. *Saved by the bell.* "I think our absence is going to awaken suspicions, especially with the visitors who've seen us messing with the library cabinet. How about we pick it up again later after the guests have gone to the cliff dwellings?"

"Okay." He glanced uneasily out the window. "Storm system's supposed to roll through later this afternoon, so I want to get them on their way as early as possible."

Deep in thought, Daniella followed him from the room. Someone was getting reckless if they'd risk tossing Sam's room with a full contingent of guests in the lodge. Plenty of people had been on the second floor around the time of their search. First Edward, then Matt and Whitney. Though she itched to examine the last snow globe, she did not hold out much hope that it contained some cache of jewels or anything else of supreme value. That would be too farfetched. Like a movie, as Sam had said. And anyway, how would gems stolen in Germany have wound up in a lodge in New Mexico without Hannah's knowledge?

She retrieved Oliver, thanking Mae for watching him, and then helped the boy get dressed. He was cheerful, eager to pack a handful of dinosaurs into a small red backpack. "For da trip," he said, holding it out.

She figured it wasn't the time to tell him that they would not be going on the excursion to the Gila Cliff Dwellings. Staying back with Zara watching Oliver would give her and Sam plenty of time to examine the last snow globe and chase down more information on the guests. While Oliver crammed in an additional half dozen dinos and a car for good measure, she texted Jodie a request to check on Edward Reese's past, the jewelry store robbery, and to see if he did actually work at an insurance company.

"Hold it right there," she said to Oliver as he reached for Nettie. "Nettie stays here."

Zara and Oliver both radiated disappointment. "Zara wants a toy," Oliver insisted.

"Zara doesn't get to take Nettie out of this room," Daniella said with conviction. "No matter what she tells you."

With a sigh, Oliver withdrew Nettie. The dog let out a half-second whine. Daniella gave her a look. "You're getting a little too spoiled around here, Zara. And is that a Goldfish cracker you're hiding in your hand for Zara, Oliver? She can't have a snack unless I tell her it's okay, remember?"

Oliver was all innocent eyebrows and chubby cheeks as he stuffed the cracker in his mouth. A preschooler and a dog were teaming up against her. She hid her smile as she marched them toward the door and out into the hallway.

The dining room had the full complement of guests. Luscious strawberry crepes were lined neatly on ceramic platters. Passing through into the kitchen, she found an extra for her and a plain waffle for Oliver had been set on the table. The location was good as she could sit with Oliver and still see through the opening into the dining room to keep tabs on the guests.

Sam was darting back and forth from dining room to kitchen replenishing the coffee carafes as the guests filled their own cups, grabbed plates of crepes and milled about. Paul and Ingrid entered through the kitchen door. They greeted Oliver and Daniella.

"We gonna make it through this adventure?" Paul asked. "Those clouds out there are thick as thieves."

Interesting simile, Daniella thought as Sam reassured them. Ingrid didn't comment, lines bracketing her mouth. She was not sitting next to her brother. He took a seat at the end of the table and sipped his coffee, picking the strawberries off the top of his crepes. Daniella made a note to get Ingrid alone if she could to see if she would let anything spill.

Whitney joined them in the kitchen and wiggled a finger at Oliver who returned the greeting. "Would you happen to have some almond milk?" she said to Mae.

Since Mae had both hands full with bowls of fried potatoes, Daniella went to the fridge and pulled out a carton for Whitney. Edward was standing behind her when she closed the fridge door.

"Almond milk for you too?" she asked.

"No," he said. "I don't think the stuff that comes out of almonds is actually milk. I need a towel." He pointed to the spot on his shirt. "Spilled my coffee and there's a puddle on the table. Sorry."

Mae set the potatoes down and fetched a dry towel from the kitchen cupboard for Edward. Daniella poured Zara a bowl of kibble and stopped Oliver from dropping a square of his waffle into the mix.

"She only eats dog food," Daniella said yet again.

Zara looked as if she thought they should put Oliver in charge of the meal planning, but she would not digress from her training. It occurred to Daniella that her partner was very much enjoying being part of a human family. The realization gave her a pang when she acknowledged that she was relishing time with Oliver and Sam just as much. There was something very natural and right about it.

Short term only, she reminded herself. After she left, Sam and Oliver and Mae would resume their lives just fine. Would she be able to do the same?

Grabbing a sponge, she washed the pots and utensils in the sink. It helped to be busy, and she could easily watch Oliver while she did so.

Finally, when her nerves were calmer, she sat down and ate half of her crepe. Too sweet for her taste, but the black coffee helped to offset the sugar. She laughed at the way Oliver lined up his waffle squares into neat rows before he ate them. Meticulous. Perhaps he'd inherited that from Hannah. The smile and restless curiosity had to have come from Sam.

Mouth suddenly dry, she downed some water.

Sam carried in an empty platter, depositing the dishes in the sink, his expression dark.

"What's wrong?" she said.

"John left me a message that he can't come today."

"Why?"

Sam glowered. "He didn't say. I tried calling him back but there was no answer. Looks like I'm going to have to take the group myself."

"No way. Not after someone knocked you down a cliff."

"There's no one else," he said helplessly.

Sam going alone? Her stomach heaved, picturing him lying still on that ferociously hot slope, unmoving.

"We can't split up. We'll go too."

He shook his head. "No, I don't want you and Oliver with us."

"Leaving us behind isn't any safer. I'm protection for you as well as Oliver. This is a drop-off only, right? They're climbing up on their own?"

He nodded. "The ranger at the ruins will handle the tour, they just need a ride. We could have tried to bundle the ruins exploration with the hike yesterday, but there's too much ground to cover in one outing."

"Okay then. We're going." She slid her breakfast away. "I'll grab my gear and be ready in five." Her gear included her weapon. There was no way she was going anywhere without that. "Good thing you packed your dinosaurs, Oliver. Looks like we are going on a trip together."

Oliver held his fork up and saluted her. She helped

him out of the chair to head upstairs to wash up and brush his teeth. As they passed the dining room, she saw that Ingrid had pushed away her plate. Angry? Worried? Riding in the lodge van would be the perfect opportunity to see if she could figure out what Ingrid had to do with the threats to Sam and Oliver. She must be connected somehow, since she had been close to Hannah in Germany. If there had been something smuggled from one country to another, she might have had a hand in it. Ingrid, Paul and Edward all had a connection to Germany. And Edward's father had lost a collection of jewelry there. Was that the key?

Her stomach cramped. *Too much coffee, Daniella. When are you going to learn?* Probably never. She'd been drinking coffee since she was a teenage runaway from her first foster home. Sunday mornings she would sneak into the services at the corner church to swipe a cup of some warm beverage from the lobby, anything really, and listen to the music emanating from inside the closed sanctuary.

In those moments she'd thought about the words to the songs, about a God who saw her and loved her, dirty and disheveled as she was. That was a father, she'd thought, the kind that would never desert you. And then God had sent her Uncle Cal, who'd helped her finally feel comfortable enough to open those sanctuary doors, showing her that God's love was not only for the well-dressed, well-homed people inside. God loved all His children, dirty or clean, poor or comfortable, in the suffering and the sunshine.

Coffee always brought back that memory to her, if she allowed it.

Ignoring the twinge in her stomach, she refocused

on her plan of attack. Time was getting short with the guests scheduled to leave in three days. She would have to put the excursion to good use, press harder to find the source of the threats.

Now or never.

Sam eyed the iron-gray clouds rolling overhead as they loaded the van. It would be a tight squeeze with five visitors, Oliver, Daniella and a Malinois, but the guests did not complain. They were fascinated with the storm gathering in the distance. He hoped the weather would hold for a few more hours at least. Desert storms could be violent and dangerous.

Daniella's face was drawn as she climbed in next to Ingrid. He thought she might have groaned as she passed him. He touched her wrist. "You okay?"

She nodded, mouth pressed in a thin, determined line.

"You sure, because—"

"I said I'm fine," she snapped.

He didn't press further.

Zara scooted in next and rolled herself into a ball underneath Oliver's car seat, which delighted his son. Oliver used his foot to scrub between Zara's ears. They'd become fast friends, those two. He thought briefly how Oliver would react when Zara left. Perhaps he should consider getting a dog to keep his son company, but it would pale in comparison to this brilliant canine.

Sad, he thought. He'd never before considered that Oliver might be lonely in the summer when he wasn't attending his preschool in Silver City or the once-a-week Sunday school class at their church. He should probably enroll his son in some sort of summer program or camp, but it was hard to transport him back and forth with the lodge duties, and there was little money to spare. What would Hannah have done to provide more social opportunities?

The miles wound by and he was so wrapped in his own thoughts, he didn't at first hear Ingrid.

"Sam," she said, louder. "Daniella's sick."

He jerked a look back. Daniella was glassy-eyed, her complexion taken on a green undertone. With one fluid movement, he pulled to a sandy shoulder of the road and put the van in Park to keep the air conditioner going. Grabbing a water bottle, he hopped out and rushed around to the passenger side. Zara yowled as they disembarked but Daniella told her to stay. Sam helped her out and hurried her away to a cluster of trees where she lost the contents of her stomach.

He guided her to a rock nestled under a pine tree and dampened a handkerchief from his pocket with the water, applying it to her forehead. He expected her to push him away, but she didn't. Her hands trembled.

Zara, crowding the floor space by Oliver's feet, shoved her head out the window, eyeing Daniella intently. If she made the slightest indication that she needed her, the dog would have barreled from the car like a furry missile.

"Thank you," she said shakily. "I don't know what's the matter with me. I felt totally fine this morning."

"When did it hit you?"

"During breakfast. I ate maybe half the crepe and then I had some coffee and felt my stomach cramp up." She arched a brow. "I thought it was the coffee, but it was probably the crepe, which was way too sweet. Odd, right? That no one else complained about their crepe being too sweet and that the cramping came on so quickly?"

Sam had a bad feeling in his own stomach just then as he considered what had likely happened. "Odd, for sure. Saw plenty of food poisoning in my day when the guys would eat at some less than sanitary places in town. Cramps, vomiting, shakiness, sweating."

Her eyes met his, a sharp suspicion gleaming there. "Someone poisoned me and added extra sugar to hide the taste. Just me, since no one else is sick."

The thought struck like a thunderbolt. If she'd been poisoned, why hadn't the others? His son? His mind pinwheeled. She'd been targeted to get her out of the way. He tamped down on the rising fury. "We'll get you to the doctor. Have Oliver checked too, and anyone else who might be feeling unwell."

She shook her head. "Oliver didn't eat what I did, so I think he's fine. Everyone else put away large portions of Mae's crepes from what I could tell, and no one else is sick. Someone likely doctored my crepes individually while I was helping with the almond milk and towels." She groaned. "Don't bother asking who. Most of the guests were in the kitchen at some point or another, except Paul and Matt, but they might have come in while I was washing dishes. But where'd the poison come from? Whoever did it would have to have access to something quick-acting unless they'd brought it along with them."

Sam considered. "I have a bottle of ipecac in the upstairs closet. If someone was snooping around, they could have spotted it."

Daniella nodded. "They knew I was planning to stay at the lodge today. They hoped to incapacitate or maybe hospitalize me to get me out of the way for a while." She snorted. "Too bad for them I have a cast-iron stomach and not much of a sweet tooth."

He felt like howling. "This is getting extreme."

"Very." She tried to get up, but he restrained her.

"We need to get you to the hospital, but you should rest for a moment, make sure the worst has passed."

She waved him off. "I only ate a few bites, so I think I'm okay."

He dabbed her temples with the water. "I am so sorry, Daniella."

She reached up and touched his hand. "Not your fault," she said.

"I feel like I should have been able to handle this... whatever it is." He could not resist stroking a finger along her cheek. "I certainly never wanted you to get hurt trying to help me."

Her gaze was soft. "I'm okay. And we're going to end this. Soon." As she finished her sentence there was a crash of distant thunder. He looked up as three raindrops splatted against his forehead and more speckled Daniella's hair. The storm had landed much earlier than forecasted. He should have been upset, but he was actually glad for the excuse to get Daniella back to the safety of the lodge where she could recuperate fully. Nor did he want Oliver on a trip with someone who'd tried to poison his nanny.

"We'll have to call off the tour anyway," he said. "Postpone until early evening. If the storm's through and we've got daylight still, we can take advantage of the cool. Still though, if you've been poisoned, I think..."

She stood, more steady now. "Not going to the hospital. If you're heading back to the lodge, so am I. Let's roll, Captain Sunshine."

"At least take my arm?" he asked.

She linked her arm with his and he guided her back to the van. He could not help but admire her bravado. His own feelings zinged between fear at what might have happened to flat-out anger. One of his guests had poisoned this intrepid woman. He hadn't felt such rage since he'd watched his wife sicken in spite of the treatments. It was one thing to knock him around, but the thought of someone targeting Daniella or his son made him see red.

"Hey," she said, putting a hand on his forearm. "Slow down, huh? And you're cutting off my circulation."

He realized he'd been speeding along, squeezing her arm in his. "Sorry. I just... I can't stand thinking that someone tried to hurt you." It might have been too much of an admission, but it was the honest truth.

She gave his arm a tug. "I appreciate that. Don't want your protection cop conking out on you right?"

He caught her eyes, those dark mirrors of intelligence and loyalty that made his breath go shallow. "Not that," he said softly. "You are so much more than your badge, Daniella."

She was silent for a moment and the soft flush on her cheeks made him realize he'd embarrassed her. Why did things come out of his mouth before they got permission from his brain? He had no idea what to say to smooth out the moment. It was awkward and overwhelming; the bold truth was that he'd come to admire very much a woman who was not his late wife.

Guilt was what he should be feeling, yet he found it was not top on his list of emotions. He filed that away to consider later.

"We need to stay focused, here," she was saying. "Let's get everyone back and settled. When the coast is clear, we can examine the last snow globe. I'll try to pump Ingrid for some information."

Now she was the one setting the pace. "How can you do all that after someone just tried to poison you?"

She gave him a glimmer of a smile. "Gotta wrap up this case before the bad guy gets away, right?"

The case. The reminder was delivered without emotion. This was a job for Daniella. Not personal. Why had he let the situation become anything else on his part? "Right," he said. "Sure." The rain pattered down on them as they returned to the van.

Daniella accepted concerned comments from the guests as she resumed her seat. "I got car sick, I guess," she said by way of an apology. "Sorry to hold everyone up." Zara greeted her with ecstatic tail wags and licks.

Sam stared at each of the guests, looking for odd expressions or a hint of surprise. Nothing jumped out at him. They were all seemingly interested in the storm. A faraway roll of thunder echoed through the trees.

"Probably good timing," Edward said. "Starting to rain."

"I say we go to the cliff dwellings anyway," Matt said. "We bought and paid for this excursion, didn't we? It's our call, right?"

"Not safe to be hiking if there's a possibility of lightning." Sam shared his idea to postpone the trip until evening, weather permitting.

The guests took the news fairly well. Except Matt.

"Just a little rain," he muttered.

But it was more than that. The clouds accumulated rapidly and the crash of distant thunder promised it would be a whopper of a storm. Sam avoided bumps and eased the van into the tight turns for Daniella's sake, which slowed them on the return. Forty-five minutes later, they made it back to the lodge. Mae held the door open for them, surprised.

"The storm got you? I was cleaning, and I didn't even realize it was raining. Weather guy says it's a big one, but I figured you'd beat it."

"The Gila is an entity unto itself," Ingrid said with a shrug. "Hopefully, I'll get to see those cliff dwellings tonight."

The guests scattered to their respective areas, most returning to their rooms for late-morning naps. Ingrid sat outside under the porch cover with Paul to track the incoming storm.

When the kitchen was empty of visitors, Daniella sat at the table with Sam, Zara at her feet, and sipped water. Her color was better, and her hand was steady on the glass. Oliver played with his dinosaurs in the corner and Mae stood, arms folded.

"We think she was poisoned," Sam explained to Mae in low tones. "Probably by the crepes."

Mae's mouth rounded into a surprised *O*. "But I cooked that meal myself," she said. "How could anyone slip something into my crepes without me knowing it?"

Any number of ways, Sam thought as he tried, without success, to soothe Mae. People who were determined to do evil would find a way no matter what the circumstances. Springing into action, Mae immediately began dumping the remaining batter, tossing the berries and swabbing the kitchen with cleanser. "By the way, John was here, and he said to apologize for not showing up."

"He was here?" Daniella said. "When?"

"About a half hour ago, before I started the vacuum. He said to tell you he had to get his sister to the clinic because she fell and sprained her ankle. He'll be unavailable for a few days."

Great, Sam thought. Then again, it might be one less person around to keep an eye on.

He jogged to the upstairs bathroom, waving to Edward, who was settled in with a book in the library. A devoted reader? Or perched there so he could watch the comings and goings of the guests, or maybe get a look into the locked case?

The bathroom yielded the answer, which he reported to Daniella back in the kitchen while Mae scrubbed the dishes with vigor. "Ipecac is gone."

"Frustrating." Daniella drummed fingers on the table. "I didn't get much from Ingrid in the van on the way back, except that she thinks very highly of you."

That caught his attention. "Me?"

She nodded. "I don't know how that fits in, but she's definitely harboring a lot of emotions about something." Daniella paused. "Paul indicated she might have had a crush on you."

"What?" His face went hot. "That's…not likely."

"Why?" Daniella said. "You're handsome, kindhearted."

Is that what Daniella thought? Handsome? Kindhearted? He felt both thrilled and awkward, like a middle-school boy. "Well, I mean… I'm not, uh, smooth, and I certainly never gave her any encouragement. My attention was always on Hannah."

"Did you spend any time with Ingrid? Help her in some way?"

He pursed his lips in thought. "I changed a flat tire and drove her to the airport once when I was visiting Hannah in college over Christmas during her junior year. One time when she was having a loud argument on the phone, I popped my head in to check on her. She gave me a thumbs-up and that was that. I never wanted her to feel like a third wheel or anything, like I was taking away her best friend."

"That might have been enough to make her fall for you."

He shifted in his chair. "But that's not romance, it's just common decency."

"Paul said she is an obsessive type. And remember how John described Ingrid and Whitney? He said they were slippery so he got some sort of bad vibe."

"But…"

She took his hand and squeezed hard. "Sam, no one, especially me, thinks you did anything to encourage Ingrid. Does that make you feel better?"

It did, for reasons he could not fully explain. Her opinion of him mattered immensely, more than it should. He scrubbed a hand over his beard. "Still doesn't make sense. If she was, er, obsessed with me, why smash me over the head or knock me down a cliff? And what does it have to do with something hidden at the lodge?"

Daniella shrugged. "Like I said, bunny trails. Do you think we can sneak into the library now? Check out the snow globe?"

Sam gritted his teeth. "No. Unfortunately, Edward's in the library at the moment. Looks like he's setting up for a long read. We'll have to wait until lunch, unless we're ready to answer questions about why we're opening up the display case again."

"He sure spends a lot of time in the library, and he's got a lot of questions," Daniella said.

"So do I," Sam breathed. They had to find answers soon. The intruder was getting bolder with each passing hour. Attacks, poisonings, room searches. Would the next attempt get someone killed? Daniella was tough, and able to take care of herself, but he could not stop worrying about her and his son. Daniella and Oliver. He'd begun to think of them as a package.

She's leaving, he reminded himself.

And that's what you want, right?

He felt like the hours ticked by in slow motion. Somehow, he forced himself to work on the laundry and secure the patio area furniture from the winds that had morphed into violent gusts. Windows rattled and the sunlight was obliterated by an ominous gloom. Edward still did not emerge from the library, though Sam made excuses to pass by every so often to check.

Daniella sat with Oliver and Zara, building block towers in a corner of the living room, while Daniella sent various texts and emails to the RMK9 Unit, trying to garner information on the guests.

The winds picked up speed, battering the lodge. Zara's ears twitched at the screeching, and Oliver jumped a few times, knocking over his blocks.

"That wind is shouting today," Daniella said.

"Uh-huh," Oliver said, smiling. "Daddy says don't shout inside."

"Gonna have to put that wind on a time-out," Sam called from inventorying the pantry, which sent Oliver and Daniella into giggles. *You haven't lost your touch, Captain Sunshine*, he thought with a surge of contentment. Contentment? A widowed guy embroiled in a plot and struggling to keep his lodge afloat didn't have the right to that feeling, now did he?

He remembered Hannah's big-belly laugh. She would tell him he was being ridiculous, as usual, and contentment was as much a part of life as grief and responsibility.

"If you don't like the path you're on," she'd say, "you got two choices. Learn to like it more, or find the new one God's got for you."

Sam'd not been allowed to step off the path that had taken them through Hannah's illness, but even that tortuous journey had taught him things he would not have learned any other way. Lessons about what was crucial in life, and how to trust God when he felt the storm of fear howling all around.

Listening to the chatter between Daniella and Oliver, he wondered if she was thinking about the child she'd given away. He hoped she felt a sense of contentment about her daughter, in spite of the pain her choice must have caused.

Eventually the clock crept to noon, and the guests began arriving at the table for lunch. Mae spread out a sandwich assembly with a variety of meats and cheeses and salads, and a platter of cookies. Apron tied around herself, she stood sentry at the table, clearly determined that no one would be tampering with any of her food a second time.

Daniella declined any lunch and made sure to prepare Oliver's meal herself. Sam was relieved. If someone wanted Daniella out of the way, perhaps they'd try the same trick on Oliver to cause more chaos. Zara was told to "watch" and she stood on alert at Oliver's knee while he ate. Someone would be foolish indeed to try and mess with Zara's charge. Again, he felt the swell of emotion seeing Daniella, Oliver and Zara grouped together.

Like a family.

"What do you think?" said a voice, breaking into his thoughts.

He realized he'd been oblivious to Edward Reese, standing next to him at the coffee station. The man looked as though he was waiting for an answer.

"Sorry, what?"

"About the storm," Edward said. "Reports say it's going to be a bad one. Will we lose power?"

"Hopefully not, but I've got a generator."

"Good to know," Edward said.

"Did you enjoy your book?"

Edward shrugged. "Mostly snoozed, to be honest."

But the two times Sam had passed by, Edward had been wide awake, not too engrossed in his book to miss Sam's progress up and down the hall.

When the entire group had finally gathered at the table, Daniella walked Oliver upstairs and tucked him in for his nap, under Zara's watchful eye. While everyone queued for the buffet, Sam sped upstairs.

He met her at the library door. "Finally," he said.

"Yeah, finally. I thought Edward would never get himself out of here."

She followed Sam to the glass case. He was fumbling through the keys while she scooted the sofa out of the way. They both noticed at the same moment. Though the case doors were closed, the small sliding lock had been removed.

And the valentine snow globe was gone.

TWELVE

Daniella smacked a hand on the sofa, her snort of disgust loud in the small space. They'd been thwarted again and the fault rested squarely on her shoulders. She should have moved the snow globe to another location to examine later, no matter how unlikely it was that something valuable was secreted inside.

Sam stood slumped, hands at his sides, which added to her guilt. How long before the intruder would get close enough to inflict real damage? Or maybe he or she had found what they'd been looking for in the snow globe and they'd slink away without facing any consequences for their actions.

"Do you think it was Edward?" Sam said. "He was in here for hours."

"Maybe. Or it could have been someone who snuck in before we left in the van." She peered closely. "The glass is pristine. I don't see any fingerprints, so they were careful."

"Do you think it means we were on the right track? That there's something valuable in that snow globe?"

"Not sure." She tried to recall the details of the ornate, red and silver globe. "Where'd it come from? Was it a gift?"

He shook his head. "No. If I remember correctly, she bought that one for herself before we started dating."

Daniella took out her phone and tapped the camera app. "The cameras probably won't help, but maybe they caught movement in the library window." She froze and looked closer at the screen. "The one capturing the side of the lodge house is down. Might have gotten jarred by the wind. I'll go check it."

Sam glanced out the window. The gusty wind whipped the panes until they rattled. "I'm coming too."

She started to protest then stopped. His lodge, his son. He had more skin in the game than she did, and it wasn't much of a security risk for him to accompany her with Zara watching over Oliver. If she was honest with herself, she just plain wanted him by her side because she enjoyed his company, more than any other man she'd ever known. What was that all about?

They made their way through the wind-ravaged courtyard where Sam stopped to secure a patio chair that had been blown on its side. The moist atmosphere felt like a sodden blanket smothering them from above. Heads bowed, they fought the onslaught and made their way to the old lodge. The camera under the eaves was tipped up, the lens pointing uselessly toward the roof. It was possible someone might have used a pole or stick to tilt the device upward to render it out of service. Or it might have been an animal scurrying under the roof, or the assault by the wind, which was especially forceful as it funneled between the two structures.

She moved to reset the camera, but Sam was already

reaching, his height making it easy for him to adjust the small unit and tighten the screws that held it in place.

"How about now?" Sam asked.

She checked her cell phone. "We're good," she said.

He heaved a sigh. "At least that was an easy problem to fix."

She double-checked the other camera views as his gaze raked the sky and the neat lines of the Cliffside. When she looked up, his mournful expression stopped her.

"I always thought of the lodge as a sanctuary, a place where I could raise my boy without the world interfering." He shook his head. There was such sadness on his face that she reached for his hand. He took it and twined their fingers together.

"We'll make it safe again." She paused and then the truth tumbled out as if pulled from her by the battering wind. "But maybe it's not so bad to let the world in. At least part of it." She'd intended to comfort, but she could not read his strange expression. He started to speak then hesitated, his eyes roving hers.

"I—I'm not sure I'm ready," he said. He squeezed her hand and then let go. "To let the world in."

Immediately the blood surged to her cheeks in a fiery blast. Had he thought she'd meant that he should let her be a part of his life? Was that actually the truth? Embarrassment tied her tongue. She'd lived her whole existence trying to keep people out. In a way, Sam had lived in the same manner since Hannah's death. Now her feelings had betrayed her. What had she done? Why had she spoken that deep-down thought aloud? She had no idea what to say.

"Sure," she said. "Of course."

"I mean…someday I know it won't be just me and

Oliver. People—others will become a part of our family. It's what Hannah would want for us, but now…" He stopped and started. "Now is just too soon maybe. Oliver's so young and I…"

"It's okay," she managed to say, willing him to stop talking. "I didn't mean to imply anything."

The silence between them grew uncomfortable.

The only possible avenue of conversation was business; the cop work, which was what she was supposed to be there for in the first place. Why had she allowed anything else? "All the other cameras look fine," she said, clearing her throat. "Ready to go back?"

His answer was drowned out by a crash of thunder. Moments later bolts of lightning began to fork down from the sky. The noise was deafening, and electricity sizzled all around.

He grabbed her arm and pulled her under the overhang, cradling her tight to his side. Her instinct was to pull away, but the cacophony overwhelmed her mortification. Another stabbing bolt slammed into a tree, dispersing in searing streaks across the ground not three feet from their location. She could not hold back a scream.

"I didn't bring my keys, and the old lodge is locked," he called over the roar. "We'll have to wait it out here."

Wait it out? Crammed next to Sam in the throes of an electrical storm was the very last place she wanted to be at the moment. She felt as if she were in the middle of a war zone. Everything in her wanted to run, but she found herself burrowing closer to his side, fear prickling her skin.

"It's okay," he said, his arms taut around her. "Just loud. We'll be all right if we shelter here."

"It makes me remember—" She gasped, interrupted by another roll of thunder. She did not want those thoughts to bubble up. Hadn't she embarrassed herself enough for one day?

"Remember what?" He leaned his face to hers so he could hear.

Lightning forked the ground, stabbing branches of light into the earth. She watched, horrified. "Living under the bleachers at the school," she said, as if the tumult around her had shaken the memory from her mouth. "That was the only time I saw a lightning storm." And this was exactly how she'd felt then, vulnerable, scared, helpless. But then she'd had no one, not the boyfriend she'd foolishly thought would love her and their baby, nor family. Uncle Cal had become her family, helped find Hope a home, and saw to it that Daniella had a place to stay until she completed the police academy eight years later.

And now she was being sheltered by a man her soul longed to know, a man who did not reciprocate her feelings. Unshed tears burned her eyelids.

"We're okay under here," Sam said. He snuggled her closer. "I'm not going to let anything hurt you."

Too late, she thought, but it was a sweet sentiment.

While the storm raged around them, she held on to those words. Sam couldn't do much about the lightning, really, but the fact that he would give his all to protect her made her melt inside in spite of her inner voice. She'd known other women to have that kind of steadfast soul in their lives, but she'd never expected to experience it herself.

Even if it was just for a moment.

Sam was not hers, nor would he ever be. She was hiccuping, trying to hold in the tears. It was like a strange, surreal dream when Sam pressed a kiss to her temple and then her cheek. The air sizzled all around them, but she could hardly feel it through the pounding of her own heartbeat. She tipped her face up to his, and he drew closer, the strong presence of him heady. He'd changed his mind, she thought incredulously. She felt him opening his heart to hers, letting go of the past that bound him. She closed her eyes, but instead of kissing her lips, he rested his forehead against hers.

"Daniella," he said. "What am I doing? I'm sorry."

Humiliation surged through her. What was he doing? And what was she? Longing to be close to a man who would always belong to another woman. He'd said it himself. *I'm not sure I'm ready.*

Either he wasn't ready or, more likely—her heart cringed—she just wasn't the one. Not a surprise. She was abrupt, hard-edged, not from the happy world of two-parent families like he and Hannah had been. That world was a place she'd watched from the outside, peeking in through the curtains at lives that were so far removed from her own experience they might as well have been fairy tales. Teeth gritted to keep from crying, she balled her hands into fists and hunched her shoulders to move as far away from his as possible. Why was she sharing snippets of her past with him? Or anyone? Allowing herself to have deep feelings for a protectee? A single father, yet.

This time, when the next flash of lightning came, she wiped her eyes and tried to straighten, inserting more distance between them. "I'm going back."

"Wait until the storm moves away a little bit."

"I'll be fine."

A bolt of lightning slammed into the pine a few yards away from the porch. The trunk exploded, hurling pieces of wood like javelins. One shot against the gutter and crushed it. In spite of her bravado, she couldn't move. Sam scooted her to the other side of the porch.

"It's moving away now. That was the worst of it," Sam said.

In trying to keep the distance between them, her foot ground against something. She looked down, another flash of lightning illuminating bits of broken glass, a gleam of red.

"What is it?" Sam reached down to pick up a shard.

Red and silver plastic stuck to the edges.

"The valentine snow globe," he said with a groan. "Someone smashed it."

"They did a thorough job." The pieces were crushed, driven into the ground, which had been hard and dry hours before.

"Do you think they found what they were looking for?" he said grimly.

She studied the fragments. "No. They probably broke it to be sure there was nothing inside. When they didn't find anything, they finished the job by stomping on it."

Sam shook his head. "And we still don't know who might have done it."

"Not really, but I'll bag the pieces and we'll send them to the lab for fingerprint analysis, to be thorough."

Sam was silent and she looked at him, waiting. She noticed he was standing a pace away from her, as if he was pained by the kiss he'd avoided a few minutes before. It was painful for her too, not to mention humiliating. She fervently wished they would both pretend it had never happened.

"I'm wondering if…" he started.

"What?"

"If we should bring in the local police."

She jerked, stung. "You don't believe I can handle it?"

"I'm sure you can, but these threats are escalating and…"

"And you think I'm not going to catch the bad guy." She was glad the darkness hid the fact that her face was molten. Bad enough he didn't want to be involved with her personally, but now her professional competence was being questioned.

"No, that's not it. You were poisoned, Daniella. Who knows what will happen next?"

"I'll protect you and Oliver," she said, jaw tight.

"I know you'll try, but I'm…"

She fired a steely gaze at him. "Afraid that I'm not up to the job?"

His voice was soft when he answered. "I was going to say I'm worried about you."

She shook her head, anger rising in untidy waves. He said it clear as anything. He didn't want her around. Suddenly, she had the desire to push for the truth, no matter what the cost, to hurt him like he'd hurt her. "Let's get it out there, Sam. You're worried that you're getting too close to me and you don't want anyone messing up the tiny world you've built for you and Oliver."

His eyebrows lifted, cheeks wet from the spattering rain. "I didn't say that."

"You don't have to. It's obvious. Being near me makes you feel like you're betraying Hannah."

His shoulders rose. "That's not true."

"I think it is. You're a straight shooter, Sam. You don't lie, except to yourself." The bitterness clung to her words.

She'd wanted to see anger in him, a wall she could beat against. Instead she saw regret.

"Daniella, I didn't mean to hurt you."

"You didn't hurt me. Offend, maybe, but not hurt," she said, trying for a careless tone.

He was quiet for a moment. "I'm not the only one who lies to themselves."

Wind snatched at her hair and she wanted to bat it from her face. "I'm here to do a job and that's all. I'll finish it, if you'll allow me to."

They stood there in the raging storm, the thunder and lightning traveling further away from the lodge. The glimmering windows of the beautiful structure glowed with a warm comfort she no longer felt. *I'm not the only one who lies to themselves.*

He reached out to her, stopping before he made contact. "I'm sorry. What can I say to make you understand that this isn't about you?"

Wasn't about her? That hurt most of all. "I think you've said enough," she said. Then she stepped off the porch into the driving rain, resolved more than ever to sniff out the intruder and get as far away from Cliffside Lodge as she could.

Sam was paralyzed for a moment before he launched himself after her. Why had he suggested bringing in the police? Was she right, that it was really more about his feelings for her than anything else?

Everything in him had urged him to kiss her, circle her in an embrace that was much more than friendly comfort. What was that? Love? Could he actually be falling for her? That was an emphatic no. Like he'd told her, he wasn't ready. Yet his growing need to share his life and Oliver's with her made no sense. And his rising sense that she might be hurt trying to defend them was out of keeping with mere friendship. In the wake of such confusion, maybe it was for the better that he'd inserted a hefty distance between them. It made logical sense to bring in the local cops, but he'd not considered that it was also a way of distancing himself from her.

Her earlier words came back to him. *You don't want anyone messing up the tiny world you've made for you and Oliver.* As he strode through the rain, he took in the neat lodge with the pristine gardens, the tidy checklists that kept the visitors going in and out, no permanent connections made, no outside influences that weren't swept away with the broom or delivered to the airport on the departure dates.

A tiny world… He'd never realized how tiny until Daniella and Zara came. Now he'd thrust her to arm's length and sent the message that he didn't even trust her to make the arrest. How had everything gone so wrong? He wasn't sure what he was going to say, but he went after her, slipping on the pine needles.

Daniella moved so fast he didn't catch up with her until he plowed into the kitchen on a blast of rain-scented wind. Paul shot him an interested look as she hustled toward the stairs. His dramatic entrance was stirring curiosity, but he was desperate to ease the hurt he'd caused. Hurt, followed by humiliation.

Brilliant, Sam. Just brilliant.

Daniella was already almost to the top of the staircase.

He took them double-time. The fourth step up, the lights went out. He froze. Though it was daytime, the storm rendered it like dusk and the lodge's small windows did not help much with illumination.

Paul's voice floated up from the downstairs living room, sardonic. "Looks like someone forgot to pay the electric bill, huh?"

Sam did not see one iota of humor. "Stay there, everyone," he said to any guest within earshot. "I'll come around with flashlights until I get the generator going." He climbed the rest of the stairs, fetched a flashlight for Daniella and tucked two more in his pockets before he poked his head into Oliver's room. Zara was watching his sleeping son and Daniella tapping at her phone.

"Is the outage due to the storm or something else?" she asked, her question formal and distant.

"Likely the storm, but I'll check the electrical box." He paused. "The generator isn't big enough to power the whole building. If it lingers, I'm going to have to move everyone downstairs."

She was still staring at her phone, making notes, nodding.

I'm sorry, he wanted to say. *I don't know how to be around you, but it kills me that I hurt you.* But she'd obviously dismissed him, and he had a crisis to deal with. He turned and closed the door to Oliver's bedroom. Moving quickly, he checked the electrical box and found it untampered with. He returned downstairs to the storage area and lugged the generator under the solid porch cover. Firing it up resulted in a low growling noise that added to the din of the storm. It wasn't going to be enough to power the whole inn. He'd meant to invest in a larger unit, but there were never any surplus funds to do so. Never enough. The words might become his life motto.

Edward appeared in the gloom from the kitchen, Ingrid by his side, dangling a tea bag in her mug. "Storm's not letting up, eh? No cliff dwelling expedition for us," Edward said.

"'Fraid not." That was the least of Sam's problems at the moment. The generator wheezed and groaned, flicking the lights in the kitchen and dining room to life.

"What if the power doesn't come back on before dark?" Whitney asked. She and Matt were seated in armchairs, holding their cell phones.

Sam swallowed. "Then we'll move you all down to the first floor to sleep, where the generator can keep the AC running and some of the lights on."

"Fantastic," Matt snapped. "That's the capper to this whole adventure. This lodge trip has been a huge disappointment. The excursion was cancelled and now there's no power. What are we supposed to do the rest of the night crammed down here together? Twiddle our fingers? Sing camp songs?"

"We have a wireless router, so you can still use the internet. The cell tower will hopefully be back online soon," Sam said.

"Hardly Sam's fault that the weather is bad," Ingrid said to Matt. "What's he supposed to do about that?"

Matt snorted. "Should have a better generator at least. Or maybe some indoor activities as a backup plan. I'd be out of here right now, except I couldn't find an earlier flight."

Whitney gasped. "What? You looked into leaving without even asking me? On our honeymoon?"

"Trouble in paradise," Paul said, teeth gleaming as he smiled.

"You shut your mouth, Paul," Matt snarled.

Ingrid shook her head at her brother. "He's right. This isn't your business."

"But it's loads of fun anyway," Paul said. "Like watching a show."

Ingrid's lips tightened. "Grow up," she muttered.

Paul's smile vanished. "I don't need advice from you, sister."

Ingrid's eyes were bright with anger. "Your life would indicate the contrary."

Paul stared back at her for a few seconds. "And you've got everything all figured out, right?"

She didn't answer.

"I feel like having a snack." Paul grabbed a lantern from the sideboard and disappeared into the feebly lit kitchen.

Sam resisted a groan. The guests were at each other's throats and things wouldn't improve the longer they sat in the half-powered inn. His optimistic side took over. Perhaps the storm would pass quickly and the electricity would be restored. Maybe Daniella would get a lead from her phone research, or a clue from the ruined snow globe.

Maybe, maybe, maybe.

Nothing had panned out so far and it felt as if the danger was howling outside along with the storm.

One of these guests was growing desperate as witnessed by the smashed snow globe. They only had a few more days before they would be forced to check out. He felt his nerves twitch.

A few more days…

But at the moment they were all imprisoned in the lodge together, and one of them was a very real threat.

THIRTEEN

Daniella's eyes burned from staring at her cell phone. Her research was notable only for what it didn't reveal. Edward Reese, supposedly on a cross-country trip, had posted zero photos on his social media. Not remarkable, since he did not appear to be very active in cyberspace. Paul and Whitney's Instagram page was crowded with images, yet that activity had ceased two days before. A side effect of their bickering?

At least the cyberwork kept her from reliving what had happened between her and Sam out in that storm. He didn't want her around and he didn't have faith that she could solve the case. Message received. But she still intended to do everything she could to solve the mystery until the guests starting checking out on Wednesday. After that, she could hand the whole thing over to the local cops, per Sam's request, and follow up while safely back at home in Denver. Depressing thought.

A text buzzed on her phone, a brief for the RMK9 Unit. Her stomach clenched as she read about the discovery of another missing woman victim.

No, not again.

This young woman had been abducted in the Green

River area of Wyoming. Same age, same physical description as the others over the past few months; a tall, blue-eyed blond. The list of names scrolled through her mind. Emery in New Mexico, Brittany in Denver, Valentina in Utah and now Elena Kimball in Wyoming.

It was possible the similarities were coincidence—there were a lot of blond, blue-eyed women in the world—but since the victims were in different states, all in wilderness areas, it appeared to be the work of a serial killer. Wes Grey, an FBI agent attached to the RKMU seemed to agree. If only those victims had been able to protect themselves, to heed some tiny instinct that might have told them to risk everything to escape their attacker. Murder was terrible, plain and simple, but when the victims were young, vulnerable women, it seemed worse. And she felt so helpless to stop any of it. Again, she felt the restless tug telling her to make a change, to turn a corner, to find a new path. She wished she could call her uncle Cal, but she didn't want to wake Oliver. Antsy, she paced the small room. Zara watched her from the bedroom with her head between her paws.

As the hours passed, there was no return of the electricity and it became too dark to remain safely on the upper floor. She, Oliver and Zara headed downstairs and set up camp in the parlor. Oliver found it to be a grand adventure and she encouraged him in that line of thinking. A cold dinner was arranged in the kitchen and the guests ate their fill before passing the hours until bedtime. It wasn't ideal, having the upper floors off limits, but there was plenty of space to provide separate sleeping areas for everyone.

The small sitting room was occupied by the honeymooners. Paul and Edward had taken over the sofas in the living room. Ingrid, the love seat in the nook by the front door. Mae would remain since it was too dangerous for her to drive home. She and Sam were still rushing around delivering blankets and pillows, long after Daniella had gotten Oliver to sleep on the parlor settee with Zara settled on his feet. It had required four dinosaur stories and two drinks of water before the boy had finally drifted off.

Sam poked his head into Oliver and Daniella's makeshift sleeping quarters in the parlor. Daniella sat in a padded chair near a small standing lamp. Zara wagged her tail at him, but did not move.

"Just added fuel to the generator. Need anything?" he asked.

She didn't look at him. "No, thank you. We're okay. Where will you sleep?"

"Not going to, probably. I need to stay on duty. Whitney and Matt wanted to leave, so I called John but he doesn't want to drive in the storm, which is probably for the best." He hesitated, about to speak again, when Mae called out. "Do we have any more pillows, Sam? Whitney needs another one."

Sam sighed. "This is going to be the longest night ever."

It felt the same to Daniella. Her armchair was not comfortable, no matter how much she repositioned. The thunderstorm continued on, sometimes reaching deafening levels. Oliver woke once, but she was able to cajole him back to sleep by singing the ABC song until his eyes closed. "Jingle Bells" and ABCs pretty much encompassed her entire kid-song repertoire, so she hoped he wouldn't wake again.

Zara yipped after a particularly loud clash of thunder,

sitting up on her haunches. Daniella started to soothe the dog then stopped. Zara was extremely noise tolerant. She'd done patrols during firework shows without a quiver. Might she be reacting to something else?

Daniella strained to hear anything amiss, but she could detect only the sheeting rain. The cameras showed nothing except a watery dark haze. Still, Zara remained alert.

"Guard," she whispered to the dog in case Zara had any ideas about following Daniella.

She pretended to be in need of the bathroom and tiptoed along through the living room, trying to see if anyone was missing. She could only make out blanketed forms. Unwilling to leave Oliver for very long, she returned to her post. Oliver was sitting up, rubbing Zara's muzzle. He turned to her and she saw that he was crying.

"Hey, sweetie. What's the matter?"

"Scary," he said, lip quivering.

"The loud noises?"

Oliver nodded.

As she went to him, she realized Sam was standing on the threshold again, apparently stopped during one of his rounds.

She looked at him, hands held up in a gesture of surrender. Oliver was not her child and she had no right to "parent" him, she'd learned the last time. This was another area she should not be involved in. Stepping aside, she cleared the way for Sam. He didn't move. A distant flash of lightning illuminated his expression for the briefest of moments. What did she see there? Sadness? Concern? Resignation? Or was there the barest hint of encouragement?

"Please," he said and stepped back out of the room.

Please? What did that mean? Oliver was sniffling now, looking as though he was ready to start wailing.

She hesitated only for one more moment before she sank down next to the settee. "Show me your 'safe' sign."

With a little coaching, he produced the sign language. "Good job. It reminds us we're okay, right?"

He nodded.

"Maybe you should show Zara, so she knows she's safe too."

Solemnly, Oliver replicated the sign for Zara. Zara leaned forward and swabbed Oliver's tears away with her tongue. Oliver giggled and lay back down. Daniella covered him with the blanket and sang the ABC song. She could feel Sam watching her as Oliver yawned and closed his eyes.

Sam swallowed as she finally turned to him and she thought there was a shine of moisture in his eyes.

"It's something, to watch your son grow to love a woman who isn't his mom." His voice broke on the last word. She wasn't sure how to reply. Love? This little boy loved her? With a painful heart squeeze, she realized she loved him too.

"I honestly didn't mean to intrude on what you wanted for your son," she whispered through the lump in her throat.

He shook his head. "It's not an intrusion. It's a blessing. I'm sorry I didn't realize it before."

She was silent for a moment. "But it hurts you because I'm not Hannah."

"It hurts because Hannah's not here. It always will. But knowing I'd kept Ollie away from people who would love him would hurt me worse. Thank you for taking care of my boy," he said.

"You're welcome."

And then he turned and vanished into the darkness.

She realized she'd been blessed and so had Sam. Both their tightly shuttered worlds had opened by the smallest of cracks. What did it mean? How would they all fare when they went their separate ways in a few more days? She did not know, and she didn't need to, not then.

At that moment, all that mattered was that she'd helped Oliver feel loved.

Just past 2:00 a.m., Zara's low woof startled her from a doze. It was still raining, but the thunder had passed. She got up and went to her dog. Zara's legs were splayed protectively across Oliver's feet. The boy slept deeply, but the dog was agitated. Straining to hear, Daniella stilled. In between bouts of howling wind, she thought she detected the noise Zara had alerted to.

There was someone moving around the upper floor. Stealthily. Sam gone to find supplies? Possible. She commanded Zara to guard the sleeping boy. Easing her weapon from the fanny pack, she quietly crept up the stairs, pausing on the landing. From there, she tried to spot the guests but it was still too dark to count heads in the makeshift sleeping areas.

Sam appeared at her elbow. "What's wrong?" he whispered.

"Heard something upstairs. Thought it might be you. I'm going to check."

"Not alone."

"Yes, alone," she said as quietly as she could. "I'm a cop, remember?"

"I'm not letting you go by yourself."

This man…he was an aggravating and enticing combination of sincerity and stubbornness. "Sam," she said evenly, "I don't want you with me on this. Go stay with Oliver."

He shook his head. "You've got two sidekicks. Zara can watch Oliver and I'll go with you."

She gritted her teeth, recalling that he did not actually trust her to handle the lodge situation. Local cops, indeed. "Don't tell me how to do my job. Turn around and go back downstairs. Now."

His exhale was intense and filled with bone-deep weariness. "Guess you'll have to arrest me then, because it's my lodge and I'm not letting you go alone."

She blinked at his bullheadedness. Not many people would stand up to Daniella's I-mean-business tone. "This is counterproductive."

"Yes, but that's the way it's gonna be, so you have to deal with it."

"Fine," she said through gritted teeth. "Can I do my job now?"

He held her gaze for three more seconds. "After you," he said gallantly.

She wanted to administer another tongue lashing at his intrusion, but instead she sighed and turned on the landing. Sam crept up silently behind her. Again, she listened to catch any movement above or below, but all was still except for the sounds of the storm.

Sam's handsome face as he'd stood up to her replayed in her mind. Handsome? Would she find herself attracted to Sam if she hadn't seen him in action as a dad? Probably. But seeing a man in the role of parent had to be one of the most crystal-clear ways to judge character. Sam was an excellent man, of that she had no doubt.

And she admired his self-deprecation, his resilience, and even his steadfast determination that his late wife would always be a part of Sam and Oliver's lives, and that was exactly as it should be. Sam was beginning to realize he didn't have to keep Oliver's world sealed and separate. It pleased her that she'd played a part in that. They'd have a good life here. A great life, as a matter of fact.

Without you.

Her spirits sagged.

Not your business, Daniella. Is it?

No matter how she felt about Oliver and Sam, they were not hers and never would be. Time to refocus.

The area at the end of the hall was an off-limits area of the lodge that led to the attic, accessible by a precariously steep staircase. She and Sam had already gone through the items stored there and found nothing of interest or significant value.

Trying to ignore the fact that Sam was crowded behind her, she eased up the remaining set of stairs. The wood creaked as they climbed. She readied her weapon and made her way on the last few rungs and into the attic. Her breath caught.

Chaos. The boxes had been dumped out, releasing a mishmash of towels, linens and bags of clothes. It was clear that someone had been using the cover of the raging storm to enact a hasty search. A wash of cool air hit her face. Signaling Sam to stay put, she jogged around a pile of old purses and a tarp-covered desk.

The tiny breeze that caressed Daniella's cheek was from an open window. She picked her way through the debris. Curtains fluttered around the sill and provided barely enough watery starlight to make the search possible. The pane of glass had been swiveled open, leading onto the tiled roof.

Using the gauzy curtain to cover her fingertips, she eased the window fully open. A quick glance showed nothing but wet tiles on the gently pitched roof below.

Daniella was puzzled. "Someone couldn't have climbed up the outside of the lodge through this window, could they?"

Sam shook his head. "No. No drainpipes or trees to use. Can't get up here except by the stairs." He sighed. "With the lights out, we wouldn't have noticed someone sneaking up here or down."

"But just now I heard movement and we didn't pass anyone on the stairs." Again she looked out into the night, but nothing revealed itself in that darkness. She'd decided to check the roof, but Sam had outguessed her. He climbed through, ignoring her angry protest.

"My lodge, remember?" He walked easily across the tiles, which pitched downward into the night. They were slick with rain. He moved closer to the edge and she resisted the urge to tell him to be careful.

"I don't see anyone," he said, "but there are a couple of broken tiles, as if—"

His words were cut off as a man's foot snaked out from behind the chimney and swept the legs out from under him.

Sam didn't even have time to cry out. Suddenly he was on his back and sliding headfirst toward the edge of the roof.

Daniella gasped and hurtled onto the slippery tiles,

grabbing for his arm. Desperately he tried to snag something—anything—to keep him from pitching over the
side. With a stab of pain, his fingers scraped uselessly
over the tiles until he managed to catch hold of the gutter. Two tiles broke off and dropped away, but it was
enough to slow him down. That and Daniella throwing
her full body weight onto his shins.

He came to a precarious halt.

"Don't move," she said through gritted teeth, her
face contorted with concentration.

"Wouldn't dream of it," he grunted. He could tell she
was trying to locate the man hiding on the roof while
keeping him from falling. Sam attempted to help, but he
didn't have a clear angle to see the person who'd taken
the legs out from under him. Whoever it was had probably scrambled away off to the far side of the roof. At
least, he prayed so, since Daniella would not be able to
protect herself while holding on to him.

Stretching as far as she was able, Daniella grabbed
the windowsill with one hand, ripping off the curtain
with the other. She let the fabric slide down toward his
torso. "Can you use the curtain like a rope to pull yourself toward me while I steady us?"

"Yes, but I don't want to take you with me if I fall.
If the weight's too much, let me go."

"Clearly," she said, her voice tight with the effort,
"you don't know me that well. Focus please."

He was beginning to think he knew her very well
indeed. As he snagged the curtain and began to try
and maneuver, he glanced at the chimney. Was there
a chance the guy was still hiding? Not much he could
do about that anyway. With every muscle straining, he
used the curtain as support to lever himself back onto

the tiles, his head toward the window again. Panting and scraping, he clawed his way until he could grasp the sill.

"That wa—"

She didn't let him finish. As soon as he was secure, she crawled quickly across the roof, freeing her gun and disappearing around the chimney. He was on his way to help her when she reappeared. "While we were busy not dying, he crossed to the other side of the roof and climbed down the drainpipe. I can just make out a deep print in the mud at the bottom."

"A man?"

She nodded. "I'm pretty sure. You?"

"I agree."

Daniella looked him over. "Are you hurt?"

"Nah. Did you strain anything by anchoring my carcass to the rooftop?"

She smiled. "No. I'm made of tough stuff."

"Agree one hundred percent." He took her hand and kissed it. "Thank you for saving my bacon."

"Anytime," she said. "But if you hadn't demanded to come, it wouldn't have happened."

"Or it could have been you dangling from the roof." He forestalled her retort with a raised palm. "I want to go make sure Oliver is okay."

She returned the gun to her fanny pack and wiped her brow with the back of her arm. "My thoughts exactly. I'll make sure the window is closed and the attic locked up until I can check it out in the daylight and make sure we haven't missed anything."

As he returned to the parlor to watch his sleeping son, Sam's thoughts throbbed along with the scrape on his elbow and myriad pulled muscles that would probably hurt exponentially worse the next day. Daniella was likely still angry at him for forcing himself into the attic expedition, he knew, but he could not help himself. Cop or not, it was impossible to picture her being hurt again. Ever since she'd been poisoned, he'd been vacillating between wanting to pull her close and detaching himself completely. What was going on in his heart and mind? He'd flat-out told her he wasn't ready to have someone else in his life and now he was interfering in her decisions. No wonder she looked ready to smack him. Daniella the Cop seemed to be morphing into softer images of her calming Oliver, snuggling against Sam's side, laughing in that rich cadence of hers.

Zara regarded him with a slight head tilt. "I don't know what to do about your partner," he whispered to the dog.

Zara rested her muzzle on her paws with a soft huff as if to say, "Don't look at me. I'm a dog."

A shout ripped through the air.

"Help!" Matt yelled. "Somebody help!"

Sam's nerves exploded.

Zara sat up rigid, legs splayed protectively over her sleeping charge. Sam rushed into the kitchen, almost colliding with Daniella as she raced down the stairs and skidded to a stop.

"What is it?" Daniella demanded.

But Matt just panted. "Hurry," he said, his eyes wild. He spun and ran back out.

Mae appeared with a blanket in her hand. "What's going on?"

He itched to ask that very question too, but Daniella put a hand on Mae's arm, looking over at Sam. "I don't know, but I need to take Zara. Stay with Oliver please," she said. She whistled for the dog.

A bleary-eyed Whitney staggered into the kitchen, a sleep mask dangling from her fingers. "Was that Matt yelling? Where did he go?"

"Stay here," Daniella commanded before she ran out into the courtyard with Zara.

After Mae's reassuring nod, Sam tore around the side of the lodge, air heavy with the scent of rain. He heard Whitney following him, breathing hard in fear. She should stay in the lodge, but he wouldn't pause for a moment to try and convince her.

"I went out for a walk and I saw her there," Matt was saying to Daniella as they cleared the corner.

Her? There? He skidded to a stop at the crumpled body on the ground. Horror warred with disbelief as he tried to process what he was seeing.

Daniella knelt next to the prostrate form. Ingrid lay pale and still, her hair splayed out across the damp earth. She looked as though she'd fallen. Slowly, his gaze crept upward. Above, where the window to the attic had been open, the curtain gleamed like a flag of surrender. It was not possible.

Ingrid looked peaceful, as if she were sleeping. Her clothes were sodden with rain.

He dropped to his knees as Daniella's fingers sought a pulse. Again, time unspooled in slow motion as he waited, not breathing until Daniella sat back. She shook her head at Sam. "I'm sorry. She's dead."

Whitney let out a cry and moved to Matt, who looked on, his face ashen, clutching his wife to his side. Whitney's sobs were muffled by her husband's chest and he patted her back mechanically, eyes still on Ingrid.

"Should I… I mean should we call the police? I got a signal a few minutes ago," Matt said.

Sam's brain felt slow and stupid. The police. Because there'd been a murder. On his property, the oasis for himself and his son. His eyes traveled to the attic window. Murder? Or had Ingrid jumped from the attic of her own accord?

"The police," Sam said faintly. "Yes." He looked around in a daze. Where was Paul? Shouldn't he have come running? And Edward?

Daniella looked at him and he read the expression there. Defeat. Call the cops when they both knew they already had one present. She—they—had not sorted things out fast enough to prevent a woman's death. He too felt the oppressive weight of failure.

Matt stepped away a few paces, still cradling Whitney, and made the call. "Yes, uh, hello, there's…a dead woman at the Cliffside Lodge." He paused. "I don't know what happened, but it looks like she fell from an upper story window."

The rest of his words petered from Sam's consciousness. Dead woman… Cliffside Lodge. A nightmare come to life.

Matt guided Whitney away from the corpse to finish his phone call.

"Zara reacted to something earlier," Daniella said when they were out of earshot, tearing her gaze away from Sam to look at Ingrid. "I didn't find anything, but it might have been Ingrid falling. She's been here for a little while, I would guess."

"Did she…?" He swallowed. "Do you think she fell, or did the guy on the roof push her?"

"I don't know. We're going to need the coroner to officially determine cause of death. She might have been working with whomever we encountered on the roof and she fell somehow. Or maybe she surprised him and he threw her off."

"Paul?"

"Let's find out." Her eyes raked the courtyard. "I don't see Paul or Edward."

"They might still be sleeping, didn't hear the ruckus."

She got to her feet, the knees of her jeans wet like his own. "I'll check. And there's no alibi for Matt either. He's the one who found Ingrid."

Matt. That hadn't occurred to him. Might Matt have killed Ingrid and pretended to discover the body? The why of it spiraled through him until he felt like shouting. Why? Why had someone chosen murder? For what purpose? To what end? It made no more sense than it had a week before when this batch of guests had arrived. Ingrid was a young woman, Hannah's friend, a teacher. She did not deserve to have her life cut short.

Daniella released a low breath. "I should have figured something out. I should have prevented this."

"We should have," he said. "There's something in my lodge that someone wants badly enough to kill for it, and I don't even know what it is."

Zara suddenly went taut, her ears pricked to attention. She let out a howl that raised the hairs on his arms.

Daniella leaped to her feet. "Sam…"

She didn't have to say it. Sam's nerves flared into terror as he understood why Zara was reacting. His son. He'd left his sleeping son with Mae.

Daniella was already sprinting to the house in Zara's wake. He pounded after her, almost overtaking them both.

The kitchen door was locked.

His fear spiked to an even higher level as he grabbed a rock from the ground.

Zara battered herself against the door.

"Tell her to get back," he shouted.

Daniella ordered Zara off. With all his force, Sam smashed the rock into one of the small panes of glass on the door, thrust his hand through, heedless of the sharp fragments, and unbolted it. He was inside in a moment, Daniella and Zara right behind him.

Daniella caught at his arm, trying to get around him. "Sam, let me…"

But no force on earth could stop him. He ran to the parlor, smacking the wall and knocking down a picture in his haste.

Oliver… Not Oliver… He could endure anything but that. In a moment, he would surely see his son curled up safe asleep under Mae's watchful eye. The truth could not be anything else. He could not endure it.

But as he pounded into the room, the bottom fell out of his soul.

Oliver's dinosaur blanket lay on the floor alongside the unoccupied settee.

Mae was gone and so was his son.

FOURTEEN

Oliver. The thought of him in a killer's hands nearly overwhelmed her senses. The side patio door was open, which indicated the abductor had taken Oliver and Mae out that way, on the other side of the lodge from where they'd found Ingrid's body. Her head spun for a moment before she gathered herself.

"Sam," she said, grabbing his arm. He looked at her, eyes hollow and burning. The tremor in his muscles transmitted up her fingertips. But what could she say? The worse had happened...she'd let it happen. He'd been right to want to bring in the local cops. Some protector.

Zara's frenzied sniffing brought her back. If they were going to save Oliver, action was needed, not self-recrimination. Whipping out her phone, she was about to dial for reinforcements when she saw the message propped on the pillow, an almost illegible scrawl on a hotel stationery pad.

The cliff dwellings. The teddy bear snow globe for your son. Call for help and he dies.

Sam pulled out of her grasp and dived forward to read it too, the tension wire-taut. "The teddy bear snow globe?" he snapped. "The cat broke that one years ago." His body was rigid with tension. "Doesn't matter." He spun on his heel and grabbed his jacket.

She reached out to stop him but he jerked away, earning a growl from Zara.

"You can't go after them, Sam."

"I can," he said, expression blazing. "And I'm going to. Oliver is all I have."

All I have. She was not sure why those words felt like a slap. "The police…" She tried.

He didn't answer, just sprinted out the front door, and she and Zara followed. Mae's car was gone from the parking lot. Sam ripped open the door of the lodge van. She barely had time to leap into the passenger side with Zara before he was speeding toward the Gila Wilderness.

"Not Matthew or Whitney unless they're both great actors. It's got to be Paul or Edward," he mumbled, hands strangling the wheel.

"Or both," she said.

He yanked a quick look at her. "They probably killed Ingrid."

She answered with a nod.

"They've got my boy and Mae."

She drew upon all her resources to force a calm tone. "They don't have much of a lead. I'm calling in the locals to update them and back us up."

He started to protest.

"I'll give us a five-minute head start, and I'll direct them to forgo lights and sirens."

His jaw was clenched tight. She had to calm him, focus his wild energy. "Tell me the layout of where we're going."

He blinked and swallowed a few times. "From the trailhead it's an hour-plus of hiking before you reach the cliff dwellings. Steep in some places. Probably mucky from the rains."

"That's good to know. They won't be able to climb all the way up with Mae and Oliver." It almost hurt to say their names, but she continued doggedly. "And they won't want to anyway. They'll need a quick escape."

His breath was still labored, but he nodded. "There's a lower formation nearer the beginning of the trail. It's steep but not too far. They'll probably hide there, ambush maybe. But there will be two of them." The fear rose in his voice again.

She gripped his forearm. "There's three of us and we're going to get Oliver back, but you need to listen to me right now."

"If you're going to try and talk me out of this, save it." His tone was savage, echoing the feeling inside her.

"I'm not, but we need to strategize." When he didn't answer, she swallowed. "I know I let you down. I was supposed to protect Oliver."

He shot out a hand and gripped her fingers hard, surprising her. "I don't hang this on you. You did your best, put yourself on the line for us. Things fell apart, that's all."

Emotion rippled through her, tears stinging her eyes. She took a long, slow breath and let it out. "I'm asking you to trust me one more time. Can you do that?" She was afraid to read hesitation in him, but she didn't. Instead he looked right at her, squeezing her fingers in his.

"I do. Completely."

She exhaled and blinked the tears away. "All right. We park a distance away, where they can't see us, and we split up."

His eyes went wide as she continued to outline her plan. His tension was palpable, but he did not interrupt. They cobbled together their scheme until they reached a spot where Sam parked the van and they continued on foot. She'd taken a coil of rope and he toted a pair of night-vision binoculars as well as a bundle they hoped would buy them some time. The moon was obscured by the storm clouds, but at least the sheeting rain had slackened. The first task was to get a vantage point to see what they were dealing with.

"Here's a good place," he said, voice hushed. Together they climbed a pinnacle of rock. At the top, the wind swirled around them, numbing her fingers. She trained binoculars along the facing cliff of rock, looking for several minutes before handing over the binoculars to Sam. "There," she whispered.

"I see," he said, voice hoarse with emotion. "The light just above that flat ledge. They're holed up there so they can see anyone approach. And I can barely make out Mae's car hidden behind some bushes at the bottom."

Sam had filled her in on the particulars. The abductor's hiding spot was a well-protected fortress off the Cliff Dweller Trail. While not connected to the ancient natural caves that had created interlinked dwellings for the Indigenous people, this solitary cave was nestled in a bluff of rugged, arid rock cocooned with ponderosa pine, Gambel oak and fir. They'd been right about the abductors choosing a spot lower in elevation than the Cliff Dwellings. A series of steplike rocks created a sort of natural staircase that had made it possible for the abductors to manhandle Mae and Oliver. The thought made her anger blaze hot.

Cool it, she told herself. *You have to be in control.*

As she scanned the terrain, Daniella knew they'd spot her in a second if she approached via the stairs. A crumbling stone cliff that jutted out adjacent to the cave set her mind in motion. If she stayed to the east-facing side and climbed up, it would put her level with the cave entrance. Sam could distract them by approaching while she readied a surprise attack. It was a wild plan, reckless probably, but she knew if they didn't act, Mae and Oliver would be killed. That would be far easier for the abductors than lugging them to the car. As soon as the kidnappers caught sight of the responding cops, they could choose to dispose of witnesses. Further, when they found out Sam did not have any jewels, his life would be forfeit as well.

After one long, silent prayer, she shared her idea. "Sam, I'm going to station Zara at the bottom of the stairs where they can't see her. She'll be ready when the time comes and I give her the signal. You get to the cave and stall."

"What will you be doing?"

"I'm going for a climb."

He started to shake his head, but she shouldered the rope. "We don't have time to argue. Too much at stake."

"I can't let you do that. He's my—"

"Your son, I know. He's also my job, but more than that…" She was dismayed when her voice broke. "I love him, too." She'd said the words softly, but he hadn't missed them.

He reached out and wrapped her in a hug, pressing a kiss to her cheek. When she tipped her head up, he found her mouth with his. "Thank you," he whispered. "No matter how this goes, I'll never forget what you've done for us."

He jogged off, leaving her trembling, butterflies circling her stomach.

Done for them? What she hadn't done was more memorable. She hadn't sniffed out the perps who'd now killed Ingrid and abducted Oliver and Mae. Definitely *had* interfered in the workings of a family and stuck in her unsolicited opinion on way too many occasions. And like it or not, she could not deny the truth that spun through her like a windstorm; she loved Sam Kavanaugh. It never should have happened, she shouldn't have allowed it to, but somehow she'd fallen hard for the single father and his little boy.

The realization thudded hard in her soul. She loved them, this family that was not hers to love. She could not have them, but at least she could leave them intact if her plan worked. Sticking to the shadows, she crept around the base of the massive jutting rock until she found a concealed spot where she commanded Zara to stay. The dog obeyed, but let out the tiniest of whines to express her concern. "I should be with you," the dog communicated clearly.

"Gotta split up if we're going to save our boy." Daniella stroked her ears. "You are the best partner I could ever have asked for." All of a sudden, she knew that this moment was a crossroads for both of them. "If we get out of this, we're going to find a new line of work, I promise."

Then she pushed her hair away from her face and started to climb.

Sam felt as if he were sleepwalking as he approached the stone stairway. Each step was a prayer, a desperate plea to God to protect Oliver and Mae. Somewhere in the darkness, an animal rustled, or perhaps it was Daniella. His heart slammed against his ribs.

What if she was hurt in the rescue attempt? He'd never met a woman who was so unflinching in her resolve to do the right thing. She was more honest than he'd been about his feelings. She was strong, beautiful, resolute, like the stone cliff he now ascended. Throat dry, he fingered the bundle he'd stuffed in his pocket before they'd exited the van. With her help, he'd wrapped a small thermos in a handkerchief, the size approximating a snow globe, they hoped.

The whole situation was simply ludicrous. All this risk and anguish and fear for some cheap decoration ruined years before that someone had presumed held a treasure. The air chilled with the ascent until his skin prickled with goose bumps. As he reached the final six steps, he heard the scuffle of movement inside. No more waiting. He wanted his son. Now.

"I'm here," he shouted, allowing his emotions to bubble up. "I'm here for Oliver and Mae. Let them go right now and I'll give you what you want."

There was a quiet scraping noise, feet crossing the gritty rock. Paul's face appeared at the cave entrance. "Did you bring the snow globe?"

Paul. Sam felt sick. Had Paul actually killed his own sister? Maybe they'd been working together and Ingrid's fall had been an accident. All Sam knew was that Paul was the one who had his son.

Instead of answering, Sam held up the bundle in his hand so Paul could see. "Send out Sam and Mae. I won't come after you."

Paul shook his head. "Come up. I want to check it."

"Give me my son first, and Mae. You don't need

them." What if Paul had already harmed them? Or worse? He was dizzy with fear.

"Get in here. Now," Paul said. "Unless you want them dead."

Dead. He thought then of Hannah and how she'd given her every breath in trying to survive so she could see Oliver grow up. When that hadn't been possible, at least she'd had the peace of mind knowing that Sam would sustain him. Now it was Sam's turn to give everything he had for the sake of his child.

He strained every sinew, praying Daniella's plan would succeed. The wind rattled the pines and chilled the back of his neck, but he heard nothing further.

Daniella, where are you? Should he call out for Zara? But if Paul was armed, he could kill the dog before she ever got close. A few more minutes. He had to give Daniella that much.

With shaking legs, he completed the final steps. Out of the corner of his eye, he saw a small cascade of debris slide from the cliff face alongside the position where he now stood. Daniella? He prayed she hadn't fallen. Pretending to stumble, he stopped for a moment, but he detected no further sound of her approach.

There was no more time to stall. After a deep breath and a final entreaty to the Lord, he climbed into the dark maw of the cave.

Daniella lost sight of Sam as he stepped into the darkness. She was now level with the entrance, her rope fixed as firmly as possible to a sharp prong of rock. Her hold was precarious on the slick and crumbly rock. From inside the cave, there was a flare of light and Daniella saw Mae holding a lantern, her arm protectively cradling Oliver.

The sight of the two made her weak with relief. They were alive and seemed to be unharmed. A new resolve filled her to the brim. God had protected them to this point and now it was up to her, Sam and Zara to finish the job. She couldn't see Zara but she had ultimate confidence that the dog was stationed and ready.

Paul stood facing Sam, who had his back to her. Daniella had a sufficient view to spot the gun in Paul's hand. As far as she could tell, it was just the four of them, no sign of Edward. Her stomach muscles tightened. Her own weapon was useless since Mae and Oliver stood in the line of fire. All right, she'd have to do things the hard way. First and foremost, she needed to be sure the captives would not be hurt when she enacted her plan.

An owl shot from the branch near her with a frightened screech. It was enough to grab Oliver's attention. Risking letting go with one hand, she waved as widely as she could at the boy. She saw in the tightening of his posture that he'd spotted her. She could only pray that Paul hadn't. Clinging to the branch with the crook of her elbow, she gave Oliver the sign language signal she'd taught him earlier for lying down. Would he understand? Was he brave enough to try it? Sweat beaded on her brow. Five seconds ticked by. It was too much to ask of the boy. She'd have to enact her plan anyway, dangerous as it was to Oliver and Mae.

Daniella was gripping the ropes when Oliver suddenly lay on the floor of the cave. Mae, concerned, knelt next to him.

It was the one moment she needed. With a surge of adrenaline, she put her fingers to her lips and whistled.

The sound pierced the night. She didn't have to see to know that Zara would receive the command and do her job. It was time for Daniella to do the same. She slid down the ropes and pushed off the rock face, hurtling feetfirst toward the cave entrance.

Sam heard the whistle and the scrambling of claws. Zara erupted into the cave, legs churning. Paul's eyes widened in terror. Without a moment's hesitation, Zara leaped at Paul, her teeth latching onto his gun arm. Paul screamed in pain and tumbled backward, the weapon firing.

Sam dove atop Mae and Oliver, sheltering them with his body from the ricocheting bullet. It pinged into the cavern ceiling, letting loose a stream of sparks before it rattled harmlessly to the floor. In a fog of disbelief, he watched Daniella swing into the cavern attached to a twirl of ropes. She freed herself and immediately dove into the fray with Paul.

She grabbed his arm below the elbow, since Zara was still clamped to his wrist. Sam rocketed to his feet and charged at Paul, going for his legs before he could kick out at Daniella or Zara. He reached up to confine Paul's other hand. The man tried to lash out a fist, but his leverage was off and Daniella knocked the gun free. Zara dove in again immediately, this time attaching herself to his pant leg. Paul continued to struggle but he was unmatched by their combined weight.

Both panting and gasping, they flipped Paul over onto his stomach. Daniella snapped on the handcuffs and called Zara off. The dog remained standing close, quivering. "You're under arrest," Daniella said, after a breath.

The fight hadn't gone out of Paul completely. "Get off me!" he bellowed.

Zara barked so ferociously that Paul stopped moving.

"Good girl, Zara," Daniella said. "Toy for you in a minute. Guard." She pointed to Oliver. The dog raced across the cavern floor and took up position near the boy, keeping a wary eye on Paul.

Sam remained kneeling on Paul, pinning his legs until Daniella pulled a second set of restraints from her pouch and fastened his ankles together. Sitting back, she wiped her brow and grinned at him. "Nice work, Captain Sunshine."

If he wasn't so winded, he would have laughed. "Right back atcha. Never seen anyone use rappelling ropes in that way."

"Skills," she said with a cocky grin that vanished quickly as she eyed the cavern. "Cops will be here soon and I'm not going to relax until we get everyone out of here." She jutted her chin toward Mae and Oliver. "I got this. Take care of them."

Sam rushed over to the two. Oliver was wide-eyed, crying so hard he was hiccuping. Zara whined, but allowed Sam to get to his son. Mae's cheek was darkened by a bruise.

Mae shook her head. "I'm sorry, Sam. I couldn't stop Paul from taking us. He said if I resisted at all he'd…" Tears streamed through the dust on her face.

"You didn't have any choice," Sam soothed, holding Oliver. "I'm glad you were here with him."

She nodded, pulling a tissue from her pocket and daubing at her cheeks. She handed another one to Sam for Oliver.

"It's all right, Ollie," he said. "The scary stuff is over

now." But the boy was breathing so fast he was beginning to hyperventilate. "Son," he said over the crying, "I'm here and so is Nanny Ella. You are safe."

It had no effect on Oliver, whose face was flushed in the dim glow of the flashlight Paul had dropped.

Daniella called out to him. "Oliver."

The boy jerked a look at her commanding tone. Zara and Daniella were both staring at the little boy. Daniella made a signal with her hands. To Sam's surprise, Oliver mimicked the sign, his cries diminishing. They repeated it several times before he calmed.

Sam looked at Daniella with wonder in his soul.

"It means 'safe,'" she said with a smile. "My colleague Jodie taught it to me and I shared it with Oliver."

"Safe," he repeated, pulling his son close. What a glorious word, he thought. One he'd never take for granted again.

"You did a great job lying down when I gave you the signal, Oliver. That's big boy stuff, for sure."

Oliver shot her a watery grin.

Daniella allowed Paul to sit up, though she kept her gun trained on him. "Cops will be here soon, Mr. Zuriya. Time to tell me about the jewels."

Paul glowered. "I'm not telling you anything." Zara barked at the angry tone, shifting uneasily, and Paul stopped talking. He also stopped moving against the restraints, sitting stiffly with his back to the cavern wall. They weren't going to get anything more from him.

Sam figured he might never know the truth about Paul's objective and he found he didn't much care. Mae, his son, and Daniella were safe, and that was enough to fill him with absolute contentment. He was rocking Oliver slowly back and forth, savoring the feeling, when Zara began to bark. After a moment of fear, he forced himself to calm down, figuring it must be the police approaching.

"I'll go—" he said, stopping short when Edward Reese climbed into the cave, red-faced and panting.

It isn't over, his mind screamed. *You let your guard down.*

But Daniella hadn't and neither had Zara. "Ready," she told the dog. Zara didn't need direction. She was already positioning her body between Edward and the others, growling as she advanced.

Edward froze, mouth falling open.

Daniella swiveled her revolver at the newcomer. "Stop right there."

Edward raised his hands, staring at Zara and then at Daniella. "I knew you weren't a nanny." He lifted his hands higher. "I'm unarmed and I'm not here to hurt anyone." He looked around Daniella at Paul. "You got him. Finally."

Finally? Who exactly was Edward Reese? Sam stood and kept a hand on his son's shoulder.

"Why are you here?" Daniella demanded. "Start talking or you'll be cuffed right next to him."

Edward did not seem to have heard. "I've been waiting a long time for this moment." He huffed out a breath before he looked at Sam. "Did you give him the jewels?"

Sam stared at him. He stared back. "Daniella was right about the jewels being hidden in the snow globe?" He shook his head.

Edward's eyebrows shot up. "Did you bring the snow globe?"

"No," Sam snapped. "I brought a handkerchief and a thermos."

Paul groaned.

"What? Then it's still at the lodge," Edward said, half turning. "We've gotta go back and—"

Daniella cut him off. "Let me make this clear for you, Edward. You're not leaving here at the moment. Local cops are on their way, and we're staying put until they arrive. Further, unless you can explain why you're here, I'm going to arrest you right now and let the cops sort it all out later."

Edward fisted his hands on his hips. "I'm not the bad guy here."

Daniella didn't quite roll her eyes but her expression said it all. "Uh-huh. You're just an honest businessman who happened to turn up at the scene of a ransom exchange asking about jewels after you've obviously been searching the lodge." She shrugged. "You tell me or you tell local PD. Your choice."

Edward sighed. "All right. I guess you deserve that much." He tried to lower his hands but a growl from Zara made him hastily raise them again. "Four years ago, Ingrid worked at my father's jewelry shop in Germany. She and her brother Paul here, cooked up a plan to steal a diamond collection Dad had on display. The theft pretty much ruined him. He couldn't get insurance for the shop after that. The stress gave him a heart attack, which crippled him. All because this greedy jerk and his sister wanted to take something that he'd never had a right to."

Paul sighed. "Save me the lecture, old man. If your dad was too stupid to secure it properly, he didn't deserve to keep it."

Edward took an angry step toward Paul, but Daniella eased closer and called off Zara. "Go on," she said to Edward, "but stay still."

"The police looked at Ingrid, but the diamonds weren't found and there wasn't enough to arrest her." Edward glared at Paul. "Nothing to prove Paul was in on it either."

Paul stayed silent. Edward's eyes lasered into him. "I'm an insurance investigator and I've spent the last four years trying to figure out how they'd done it and what happened to the gems," Edward said. "I knew they hadn't cashed in on the diamonds, from what I could tell. No upgrades in lifestyle. No rumblings from fencers, and they would have had to contact someone like that to unload them. I kept tabs on them with no luck until just this month when I became aware that they were traveling to the US, to the Cliffside Lodge to be specific, the place Ingrid's college roommate lived. That was too much of a coincidence and it got me to thinking. Ingrid and her half brother didn't get along well, so why would they vacation together? And why at Hannah's place?"

"Certainly not for pleasure," Paul said, breaking his silence. "No one annoyed me like Ingrid."

"That why you killed her?" Sam said. "Your own sister?"

"Half sister, and I didn't plan to. When we couldn't find the diamonds in the attic, she wanted to forget the whole thing. She was mad at me for scaring the kid too. The disagreement got ugly. It was always her way or the highway." He shrugged. "Things got out of hand and I snapped and shoved her out the window. She slipped off the roof."

Sam could do no more than shake his head and take a look at his son. Oliver was calm, watching Zara and Daniella. Mae seemed all right, pale and shaken, so he urged her to sit on a rock. "You're both in for a disappointment, Edward." Sam said. "There are no diamonds in the lodge. If there were, I would've found them, or Daniella would have. I never would have let my family endure all this risk for any amount of treasure. You did all this, caused all this damage for nothing."

"Two million dollars worth of gems is not nothing," Paul said. He sighed. "It really was the perfect plan. We hid it in the bottom of a snow globe."

Edward nodded. "I figured it had to be stowed in some collectible, and the snow globes fit the bill."

Paul smirked. "Ingrid knew Hannah was moving to the States, so she figured she'd stash it in something of Hannah's for transporting it, since they couldn't hope to fence it in Germany with the police on the alert."

Edward glared at Paul. "My dad hired private investigators so they knew they were being watched."

"That's right, Sherlock," Paul said. "The stash would be flown to the US, far away from any investigation, and Ingrid could retrieve it at her leisure. Who would suspect a dear college chum showing up for a friendly visit? Easier to find someone to fence it for her in the States too."

Sam sighed and resisted the urge to slap his forehead. "I remember Hannah saying Ingrid contacted her several times to arrange a visit, but with the lodge remodeling, a new baby, then the cancer, we had to close things down for a while, so Ingrid couldn't find an excuse to come retrieve it."

"Until now, which is why I kept a close eye on

them at the lodge." Edward sighed. "I watched Ingrid, searched everything in the library and all the snow globes in your display case. I couldn't get the bottom off the valentine one, so I took it to the old lodge, looking for some tools and privacy to crack it open, but I dropped it." He looked at Paul. "Which snow globe did you hide them in?"

Paul sneered at Edward. "Why should I tell you?"

Sam turned to Edward. "The teddy bear snow globe, according to Paul's note." He stroked Oliver's hair. "But I hate to tell you that it broke years ago. If we'd found diamonds pouring out of it, we'd have turned them over to the police."

Edward blanched. "You mean the snowglobe's gone?"

Sam nodded. "Yep."

Edward sagged and Paul laughed.

Again, Daniella stopped Edward from advancing on Paul. "Edward, stay put. I hear sirens. We'll let the local PD sort this all out." Her gaze shifted to Sam. "I think we've got the important stuff handled, right?"

Sam locked Oliver in his arms, fighting against emotion.

"Yes," he said. "We sure do."

He shoved the wrapped thermos into his pocket. The diamonds were gone, along with that snow globe, years before. No more danger, no more fear.

And no more Daniella?

As he looked at her, he knew there was one more very important thing that was left undone, but it might be the hardest matter of all to set right.

FIFTEEN

Soon the sound of booted feet on the rocky steps alerted Daniella that the police were at hand. She called Zara off as two officers rushed in, and gave her the rubber ball she kept in her pouch as a reward. Daniella filled the cops in with a cursory rundown while Zara chomped on it. They looked as astonished as Daniella felt as the gem-smuggling story was revealed.

"What do we do with this one?" a female officer said, jutting her chin at Edward.

Daniella shrugged. "I'd say he's a person of interest until we can check out his story. Take him in too."

Edward's voice was desperate. "All right. I can handle a trip to the station, but think. Maybe the broken snow globe is still boxed up somewhere. If those diamonds are found while I'm gone—"

"You'll be the first to know," Sam finished. "Or maybe the second."

Daniella could tell by the flippant remark that Sam didn't care one whit about the diamonds. She didn't much care either, except that it was the remaining thread in the case that would leave her forever wondering.

"And by the way," Sam said to Edward. "When you are released, you're no longer welcome as a guest."

"Me?" Edward looked honestly surprised. "I didn't steal anything."

"Your sneaking around added to the danger to my family. You didn't see fit to share with me that there was a thief under my roof and you didn't come forward when Ingrid was killed. Like I said, you're no longer welcome."

Edward followed the officer out of the cave without further comment.

The second officer unfastened Paul's legs and guided him out of the cavern as well.

Daniella rejoined the others and again tossed the ball for Zara when she brought it back. "Want to throw it this time, Oliver?"

He nodded and laughed as Zara scampered to retrieve it.

"Ready to go home?" Sam asked Mae and Oliver.

"Ready is an understatement," Mae said as Daniella took her arm. She had already declined the officer's offer to bring in a medic. "The only favor I need is to be dropped off at my home for a hot shower and a good night's sleep." She hesitated. "If you're sure you'll be okay alone for a night."

"They won't be alone," Daniella said before she could rethink it. "I mean I'll be there for another night at least." She did not meet Sam's eyes. It was going to be hard enough to leave without a whole landslide of emotion added in.

Oliver noticed a small scrape on his finger, and he began to whimper. Nothing to do with the owie, Daniella surmised, but more with the terrifying experience he'd just endured. Zara was at his side in an instant, swabbing the wound with her tongue until Oliver was laughing once more.

Daniella didn't stop the dog and neither did Sam. "Not the best disinfectant," she said.

"But maybe the perfect medicine." Sam watched Oliver grin as he fished in the pocket of his pajamas and produced a Goldfish cracker.

"What did we say about people food for dogs?" Daniella said, smiling.

"Just one?" Oliver asked.

"Okay," she agreed. "Zara's done good work tonight, so I guess one Goldfish won't hurt." Daniella gave Zara the okay.

Zara gulped down the treat in an instant, licking Oliver's fingers for good measure.

Sam took Oliver in his arms. "Ready to go home, son?"

Oliver nodded. "Nanny Ella and Zara too?"

Sam looked to Daniella. She swallowed. "Sure." It wasn't the time to tell the boy they'd be leaving as soon as the police finished interviewing Edward and booking Paul for the abduction of Mae and Oliver and his half sister's murder at the minimum.

"And Mae?"

Mae hugged him. "I'll be there tomorrow, and we'll do some finger painting, okay?" She stood close, protectively, still sniffling. Haloed by the weak starlight that filtered in through the mouth of the cave, they looked like a family; father, son and grandma drawn together in that circle of silver.

And Daniella stood in shadow, watching something play out that she was not part of. It had been sweet and precious, she realized, to love a child again. Her own daughter she'd only been able to mother for a few moments, and this boy...well, maybe she'd never really mothered him at all. Somehow though, she'd managed to love him. Her heart squeezed. And, like her daughter, she'd leave him because that's what was best, what was right for him and his father.

Pain cleaved her heart. A new path, she thought. God had brought her to this wild place and showed her that she was capable of love, even though it wasn't going to remain in her life. The lesson was excruciating, but she would not flinch from it.

I'll miss you, Sam, she thought, *and Mae and Oliver and this place.* But she would never be sorry for a single moment. After a steadying breath, she followed them out of the ancient hollow of rock, leaving the final details to the local cops.

Sam wasn't entirely surprised to find that Matt and Whitney were already gone from the lodge when they returned. He found the text they'd sent.

We went to a hotel in Silver Springs after we talked to the cops. Too many bad memories here. Police told us you are all safe. Happy to hear it. Take care.

He didn't exactly blame them. The police had removed Ingrid's body, but were still photographing and bustling around. Bad memories for sure.

And there remained the matter of the phantom diamonds that had led to murder and abduction, yet there were no more snow globes to be searched. If it had been the teddy bear snow globe, it was long gone. Diamonds.

The idea was still ludicrous to Sam's way of thinking. No sparkling stone was worth living a lie or even committing a murder for. He could hardly process through his profound relief that Oliver and Mae and Daniella were alive and unharmed.

He helped Oliver slide under the covers.

"Are there diamonds, Daddy?"

Sam laughed. "I don't think so, son. I've cleaned this lodge from top to bottom, and the only gem I ever found was a pearl earring that one of the guests lost."

Sam selected a stack of Oliver's favorite dinosaur books.

Daniella came in and sat quietly in the rocking chair. Zara took up her position at the foot of Oliver's bed. The boy had insisted that Nanny Ella and the dog sleep in his room as they'd been doing for a week. Sam dreaded explaining to Oliver the next day that his nanny and her furry companion might be leaving, if his plan didn't work. The thought seemed to prick and poke at the tenderest places in his heart.

While Oliver considered which book he wanted for story time, Sam moved closer to Daniella.

"Paul admitted to everything, including pushing Ingrid out the window, though he insisted to local police that he didn't actually intend to kill her. He poisoned me with ipecac, and shoved you over the wall at the Gila overlook, and tried to knock you off the roof when we almost caught him in the attic," she said in a whisper. "He also told them he'd shoved you when you almost found him searching the outbuilding before I was assigned the case."

"He was the one in the screen room, too, right? And responsible for ransacking my room?"

She nodded. "Or maybe it was Ingrid. I think she wanted to forget the whole thing after a while, but Paul wouldn't allow it."

"If Hannah hadn't gotten sick, she would have come to visit and found out the teddy bear snow globe was already broken. Those diamonds are in a dump somewhere." He sighed. "I wonder if they'll ever be found."

"I hope so, for Edward's sake."

"This one," Oliver announced, waving a book.

"Okay, but Zara's gonna have to move over so I can sit on the bed," Sam said with a chuckle. The dog obligingly eased toward the wall and Sam settled on the edge.

Mechanically, he read the story. Oliver's eyes were at half-mast when he finished. "Turn on the song, Daddy," his son requested sleepily.

Sam reached for the wooden box and froze, his fingers halfway there.

Daniella was instantly alert. "What?"

"That snow globe that broke? It had a little scene with bears inside and it played a tune. Hannah found it in pieces and cried because it was one of her favorites. She cleaned it up and threw it away. But I—" he swallowed "—can't believe I didn't remember before."

Daniella was at his side now. "You what, Sam?"

"I saved the musical part and built it into a box. Hannah started the bedtime ritual of winding it up every night for Oliver." Fingers shaking, he turned the box over. Daniella handed him a penknife from her pocket and he pried open the bottom and undid the screws he'd used to fasten the mechanism in place. The metal contraption came loose. He held it to his ear and shook it. "I don't hear any jewels rattling around in there. Maybe I'm wrong."

"Is there a way to open it?"

He slid the blade of the knife under a seam and the bottom detached from the top. "I don't see anything..." he said, peering inside. "I—" Then he stopped. Wedged into a crack behind the crank was a small piece of felt. He used the knife to pull it loose. Holding it over the bedside table, he carefully unrolled it to reveal four glittering pea-sized stones.

"Diamonds, Daddy?" Oliver asked sleepily.

"Diamonds," Sam said, incredulous. "They were there all the time." He wasn't sure whether to laugh or cry. "So this is what Paul and Edward were both looking for."

"And Ingrid. She just wasn't as bloodthirsty as her brother."

He stared at the sparkling pile of gems. "If I wasn't looking at it with my own eyes, I never would have believed it."

Daniella reached by him and photographed the diamonds with her phone, before she retrieved a plastic bag and slid the felt and jewels inside. "I'll get these to the cops, right now," she said. "I'll be gone for a while."

When Oliver started to protest, she pointed to Sam. "Don't worry. Dad's going to be right there with you every moment. Remember?"

Satisfied, Oliver settled back on his pillow.

Sam wanted to say something to Daniella before she left, but he couldn't seem to get started. She appeared suddenly detached and business-like, perhaps to prepare them both for her departure the next day.

He watched his son sleep, soul-weary but deeply grateful.

The nighttime passed in a blur. Sam slept on and off,

Oliver within easy reach. Even so, his son woke up several times crying. "Nanny Ella and Zara," he'd wailed.

When Daniella had returned from the police station, she'd checked in on him and Oliver, opting to sleep in the empty guest room down the hall and taking Zara with her.

Sam had sufficiently soothed the boy for him to return to sleep, but Sam's thoughts stampeded in unruly circles. Edward, who'd agreed to stay in town after his police debrief, was elated that the gems had been found, but booked lodging elsewhere at Sam's insistence. He needed to have everyone check out, so he could regroup.

What did that mean, exactly? Should he return to the mind-numbing cycle of days and nights, the excruciating effort of trying to keep Oliver in a cage of memories he could not experience for himself? Or should he act upon his brash idea?

Lord, why is my heart yearning for Daniella? Love or friendship? Gratitude or devotion?

The answer was clear as the sky after a desert storm. Unexpected as it was, he loved Daniella, with as much depth and commitment as he'd loved his late wife. Breathless, he waited for the rush of guilt that should accompany the thought, but it didn't come. Instead he felt only sorrow that if she did not feel the same, she would be leaving.

"Lord," he whispered over the head of his sleeping son. "If this is not Your will, please help me to see that." Heart pounding, he counted the minutes tick by until dawn, images of Daniella rippling through his consciousness.

The next morning she placed an early call to Tyson and the team and announced her retirement.

For a moment, there was dead silence and her stomach flipped at their expressions. She'd dropped a bomb, that was for sure. Jodie Chen recovered the quickest, probably because she'd called her beforehand.

"We're really going to miss you and Zara," she said.

The hitch in Jodie's voice made a lump form in Daniella's. As tremulous as she felt, she knew it was the right decision for her and her dog. "Thanks, everyone," she mumbled.

Officer Reece Campbell shoved back his unruly dark hair. "Takes a lot of guts to make a u-turn in your life. You, uh, sure about this?"

Was she sure about turning her back on the only thing she'd ever been good at? Zara seemed to sense her emotions and she laid her head on Daniella's thigh as if to say, "You got this, Mom." She blinked back tears. "Yes. I'm sure."

Tyson's gaze burned through the screen. "Then we'll respect your decision, though we need every good cop we can get right now."

"You'll crack the Baby Chloe case, I know you will."

Reece spoke up again. "Kate Montgomery has been moved to a rehab center, so hopefully her memory of the vehicle fire and why she'd had Chloe in her car will come back to her."

Daniella found her hands were tensed into fists in her lap. It would be hard to separate herself from the case, but she knew Reece and the others would not rest until the baby was returned.

Wes Grey, attending the meeting remotely from his FBI office in Cheyenne, didn't speak, but she saw his mouth pinch, no doubt thinking about the other issue with which the team was wrestling, the serial killer murdering women in wilderness areas.

"If there's anything I can do to help, just shout," Daniella said, forcing a light tone. After she signed off, she stroked Zara's ears. "Well girl, I did it. Time to start a new life now."

Just the two of them again, she thought with a pang, as alone as the day she'd arrived at the Lodge.

Sam found her right after dawn sitting with Zara in the courtyard where Ingrid had died. He'd probably never be able to forget what had happened to the poor woman there, but the next few minutes were all about the future not the past. Resolutely, he joined her as she gazed up at the Creamsicle sunrise.

"Penny for your thoughts," he said, his stomach fluttering with nerves.

She smiled. "They might not be worth a penny." Both their gazes were drawn to the fountain of glorious morning color emerging over the crags. They were quiet for a few moments.

"I haven't had a chance to thank you for saving my son, and for ending the insanity taking place here," Sam said.

"I should have figured it out sooner. Paul and Ingrid were the connections to Hannah from Germany."

"Bunny trails, like you said."

She sighed. "I think I'm done with bunny trails for a while."

Surprising. "Yeah?"

"Yes. I've decided that it's time for me to step away from police work. Zara is eight years old and at the very beginning stages of arthritis in her back legs. She needs to retire and I want to spend more time with my uncle." She pulled in a breath. "I have a natural tendency to put up walls and police work only encourages that. Being here, I dunno, reminded me that there's another way to live. I want to grab hold of that before I forget the lesson."

Delight flowed through him as she continued.

"The team's getting closer to cracking open the Baby Chloe case." She'd told him a little about the cases the RMK9 Unit was working on while she was there. "They'll find that baby, God willing."

She flicked a glance at him. "And now it looks like this matter is all wrapped up, too. The diamonds will be returned and the insurance matters all settled, eventually. Edward had the satisfaction of knowing Paul's going to prison. At least he can give his father that." She tossed the ball for Zara, who scampered off to get it. "Nothing stopping you from returning to your regularly scheduled life, Mr. Kavanaugh," she said lightly.

He cleared his throat. "Yes, there is. My regularly scheduled life has been interrupted and it will never be the same."

She looked startled. "Sorry about that, but it all ended well, right?"

"I'm not sorry. I'm ecstatic."

"Well yes," she said cautiously. "Oliver was unharmed."

"And I'll always be overwhelmed with gratitude about that. But I've been given another blessing too."

"Knowing you found the diamonds?"

"No, something better. God thumped me hard on the back and made me recognize that I was stifling two lives, my son's and mine." He took her hand. "I was trying so hard to hold on to memories because I thought that was all I had left. I lost sight of the fact that I have my son and Hannah will always be a part of both of us, no matter what Oliver does or doesn't remember about her."

She offered a half smile. "That's good, Sam. I'm happy for you. It's all so unbelievable what's happened here. A little excitement goes a long way." She looked down at their linked fingers and tried to draw away but he wouldn't let her.

"It's not excitement, it's love."

Her eyes widened and he felt her body go stiff with surprise.

"What?"

"Love. I love you, Daniella."

"No," she said slowly. "You don't. You're just grateful, that's all. That's not the same thing."

"I'm old enough to know the difference."

But she'd pulled away from him and was marching off toward the house, whistling to Zara. "Come on, girl. We gotta go."

He caught up and gently put a hand on her shoulder. "Don't run away from this."

She whirled, her eyes glittering. "Look, I appreciate the sentiment, but we've only known each other for a week and…"

"And that week has pushed me to my absolute limit. I almost lost my own life, my son's, and I watched you in danger, poisoned. A woman was murdered right here on my property. That's something that gives a person perspective." He took a breath. "I also saw you put everything on the line for me and Oliver, and don't tell me that was all your job, because it wasn't. You have become the world to both of us."

There was a tiny tremor in her chin, which gave him hope.

"What do you want me to say?"

"Tell me the truth. You love Oliver, don't you?"

After a long pause, she finally answered. "Yes."

He smiled. "All right. Then that leaves only one more question. I don't want to play games and I don't want to waste time. I've done enough of that already. I love you, Daniella. I want to know if you feel the same. If you don't… I'll stop talking and let you pack up and leave."

She tipped her head away, but he guided her chin back so she had to look at him. "I love the woman you are, strong, sweet, sassy, faithful, stubborn."

Her lips pursed, as if she would speak. Half afraid of what she would say, he had to finish. "And you've made me realize that Hannah would want that kind of love for me and for Oliver."

A breeze toyed with her hair, the moment long and full of uncertainty. Maybe the longest moment of his life.

"I can't step into her place," Daniella said, so low he almost didn't hear.

"I'm not asking you to. I want you to make your own place in a family…my family, with me and Sam and Mae."

The tears flowed down her cheeks unchecked. "I had a child and I gave her away."

His fingers traced the progress of one warm tear. "And that hurt you to the core, but it was the right decision, for her and for you. It's a lot to ask you to step into Oliver's life and be a part of raising him, but I'm hoping you'll make another unselfish decision and help me parent him, love him, as much as I do."

"I'm not Hannah," she gasped, voice wobbling. Zara poked her nose at Daniella's knee in concern.

"No, you're not Hannah. You're Daniella, the woman

I love and I want to marry." When she didn't answer, he rushed on. "If you need a long engagement, that's fine with me." He'd pushed too hard, too fast.

She gulped. "I don't know what to say."

Say you love me too, his heart pleaded. But she remained silent. "Hold on. There's something missing here." He waved to the house and Mae brought Oliver out. Oliver raced over as fast as his short legs would carry him, flung himself to his knees and took the ball Zara dropped. He tossed it, grinning, as Zara raced off to fetch it.

"Oliver," Sam said carefully, taking a knee next to his son. "I know you don't remember your mommy well, but she loved you very much."

Oliver's eyes were still on Zara as she plunged into the bushes to retrieve her ball.

"But you know what I think, son?"

Oliver looked at his dad now, the inquisitive arch to his brow so like his mother's. Sam blinked against tears, allowing the feeling of peace to flow through him, confirming his prayers had been answered. "I think God can send us other people to love us, since Mommy is not here. Do you think that's okay?"

Oliver nodded. "Uh-huh." He looked at Daniella. "Want to be my mommy?"

The little boy was so sincere, his expression so guileless, that Sam felt a lump in his throat.

"I… I'm not sure," Daniella said, voice hoarse. "Do you…want me and Zara to stay?"

Oliver tipped his face to the moonlight and then he wrapped his arms around Daniella's leg. "Uh-huh," he said, his voice muffled by her jeans. "I love you. And Zara."

Daniella reached down to caress his hair, her expression a mixture of pleasure and pain. "I love you too," she choked out.

Oliver released her and went to take the ball Zara had finally returned.

Sam stayed on his knee and reached for Daniella's hand. "I love you," he said again. "Do you think… I mean…do you feel at all like you could love me too?"

Daniella stayed quiet so long that a wiggle of concern started up inside him.

"I don't know," she said. "You're distracted all the time, and you don't know anything about dogs, and I don't like your taste in music one bit."

He smiled then and so did she.

"But yes. I didn't want to fall in love with you or Oliver or…" She waved her hand around. "This place. But I did and I do. I love you, Captain Sunshine."

He laughed, a long hearty guffaw that lifted his joy into the desert sky.

"So you'll marry me, Daniella?"

"That's an affirmative," she said.

He jumped to his feet. "Permission to hug, Zara?"

The dog took her cue from Daniella and sat down to play with her ball.

Sam wrapped Daniella in a bear hug that lifted her from the ground. Gilded by sunlight, they held on to each other and it felt to Sam like he'd turned onto a wonderful new path, Daniella, Oliver and Zara by his side.

* * * * *

Don't miss Harlow Zane's story,
Defending from Danger, *and the rest of the*
Rocky Mountain K-9 Unit series:

Dear Reader,

We've been on a wild ride so far in this Rocky Mountain K-9 series, haven't we? As the search for the missing baby continues, it's been a pleasure to get to know Officer Daniella Vargas more deeply. The past has a strong hold on Daniella, as it does on us sometimes too. We hang on to our failures, the hurts inflicted on us and by us, and there is no escaping the history we've created for ourselves…except through the Lord. He knows. He forgives. He binds up our wounds with understanding and deep compassion. Isn't that a comforting thought?

I hope you will continue on with the next books in the series. If you'd like to connect with me, feel free to visit my website at www.danamentink.com. There's a physical address there if you'd like to reach out by mail and I have a sign up for my newsletter, which is filled with goodies and giveaways. You can also find me on Bookbub and I have a Dana Mentink Reader Facebook page as well. God bless you, dear readers!

Sincerely,

Dana Mentink

LOVE INSPIRED

Stories to uplift and inspire

Fall in love with Love Inspired—
inspirational and uplifting stories of faith
and hope. Find strength and comfort in
the bonds of friendship and community.
Revel in the warmth of possibility and the
promise of new beginnings.

Sign up for the Love Inspired newsletter
at **LoveInspired.com** to be the first
to find out about upcoming titles,
special promotions and exclusive content.

CONNECT WITH US AT:

 Facebook.com/LoveInspiredBooks

Twitter.com/LoveInspiredBks